Wire & Word

A Vatican AI Thriller

Victoria Michael

For the questioners

PART I: WHOSE VOICE?

CHAPTER 1

The Pope's hand, mottled and blue, rested on the gilded armrest. One by one the cardinals bent to kiss the ring, lips recoiling as if from heat.

Chairs scraped. They settled like chessmen, nods traded, whispers knitting into urgency.

Cardinal O'Connor called the meeting to order. The heavyset Boston prelate turned to the Pope. "Holy Father, we've brought someone who can help us speak to the faithful. Mr. Ethan Cross, from California."

Cross was neatly tended, hair precise, smile practiced, but an alertness in his eyes felt less stagey than survival. He shone among the princes of the Church and pitched his voice just shy of reverence.

"Our children listen to their screens more than to us," he said. "What if we met them there without surrendering what's sacred? I've brought something that can make the Word feel immediate again."

He placed a small black speaker on the table, no larger than a prayer book.

Up close, the polish had hairline cracks. As he set the device down, a flash cut through the room: chain-link at a Central Valley high school, wax puddled where wind had bullied candles flat, a boy's photo gone soft at the edges. Ethan's fingers found the knot of his tie and tightened as if on instinct; then the smile came back, practiced and bright, and he went on.

"An AI," he added more quietly, "trained on scripture, and the Church's own treasury of approved texts. It can pray with anyone, anywhere. Ask."

The Chilean cardinal, who oversaw South America's fastest-growing dioceses, hesitated. "Lord, teach me to pray," he murmured.

The answer came measured, inevitable, recognizable before it was understood. Each phrase landed with the gravity of chant. The men leaned in. A collective breath went out.

The Chilean spoke first, setting a tablet on the marble and tapping a map bright with red pins. "Hotspots: Brazil, the United States, the Philippines." His thumb circled them; a pleased murmur went round. "Mass attendance up eighteen percent where we've tested this."

Cardinal Schumacher, whose German diocese had closed twelve parishes in five years, studied the tablet's statistics with the focus of an accountant. When Cross mentioned engagement metrics, Schumacher's eyes sharpened.

"How sustainable?" he asked. "Long-term retention, not just initial downloads." Cologne's empty pews haunted every decision he made.

Across the table, Cardinal O'Connor leaned forward with different energy entirely. The Boston prelate had built his reputation on spiritual renewal: parishes where healing services drew crowds again. To him, Cross's demonstration felt familiar: another vessel for divine encounter.

"The testimonials," O'Connor said, voice warming. "Tell us about the personal transformations. The Spirit moves through new channels in every age."

Schumacher's mouth tightened almost imperceptibly. "The Spirit," he said quietly, "needs to fill pews as well as hearts."

The Pope lifted a trembling hand in blessing. "Now the Church will speak again," he said, and fell into a coughing fit.

Several cardinals exchanged quick, satisfied looks. One smoothed his cassock as if laying down a winning card.

Outside the heavy doors, the cough carried down the corridor of the Apostolic Palace. A gaunt friar waited there, robed in rough grey-blue, sandaled feet cracked with chilblains, fasting having pared him to the rope at his waist.

Eye to the keyhole, he saw faces alight with wonder. He saw the black box. He saw the polished man who had brought it. His heart knotted into prayer. He lingered in shadow, ready to wheel the Holy Father away from what he judged a sacrilege.

CHAPTER 2

Daniel's Beacon Hill brownstone still looked expensive, though now it felt like a mausoleum. Unopened envelopes covered the parquet floor; gaslight from the streets flickered against dishes stacked in the sink; clothes draped carelessly across chairs. The Tesla in the garage hadn't moved in weeks; down at Charlestown, the Bayliner was tarpaulined. Once trophies, now anchors, they dragged him steadily toward insolvency.

He opened the bank app, watched the retainer clear the account, and shut the screen with a breath that tasted faintly of resignation. Each invoice could have paid months of groceries, but he could not risk losing legal protection. Nexus's lawyers were still circling.

He slumped into the Italian leather couch he'd bought with his first bonus, scrolling Blind, the confessional app for the broken, burned-out, and disillusioned of big tech. It was a trading pit of gossip, layoffs, and smoke-and-mirrors AI. His thumb kept flicking the feed; his eyes skimmed headlines with the same flat intensity as a sleepwalker.

His laptop lay open beside him, the screen showing his seventeenth rejection email. *Thank you for your interest, but we've decided to move forward with other candidates.* He'd started at senior roles, then regular developer positions, then anything remotely technical. The last rejection had been for a junior role he could have done in his sleep five years ago.

The memory hit as it always did: the sterile conference room, the water in cans, and the packet as thick as a mediocre novel. He'd signed the Mutual Separation Agreement, a paragraph in dense legalese that translated to: should any future remarks cause harm to Nexus's brand or valuation, we will end your life in court. His badge had gone slack in his pocket, a small death of access. Two days later, the certified letter arrived: *Notice of Intent to Pursue Damages*. Damages plus interest equals a boat sold, a car let go, a house that would not be a house much longer.

All of it was because of principle. *Screw principle,* he thought, drinking from a warm can of Coke.

His phone buzzed. Another bill notification. He let it buzz out. He remembered texting the one colleague who might still answer: *Coffee? No agenda.* The reply: *You're radioactive, man. I'm sorry.*

The next notification made him pause. An email, not from a creditor or another rejection. The sender was Ethan Cross. The celebrated entrepreneur, all evangelical polish. Daniel distrusted that whole orbit, yet desperation made him read: *Looking for a lead developer... Your*

uncompromising view on ethics makes you essential…
Maybe a chance to start afresh in Europe…

Europe. A place where no one knew his name. Where he wouldn't wake up each morning to the suffocating weight of being Daniel Morrison, the whistleblower who threw his career away.

He looked around the apartment, the debris of neglect covering the cumbersome trophies of his corporate life. All of it beautiful, all of it bleeding him dry. Really, nothing kept him in America at all.

He clicked reply, not because Europe was clean, but because he was running out of ways to fix the big things and hadn't yet remembered how to fix the small ones. That night he fell asleep on the couch, shoes on, with the letter from Legal on his chest like a page from scripture you didn't believe but couldn't ignore.

CHAPTER 3

The newsroom smelled of burned coffee and printer toner, the January light outside dull against the Potomac. Phones trilled, keyboards clattered, wires hummed in their racks. Bill Reilly sat slouched at his desk, sleeves rolled, tie hanging loose. He scrolled wire copy with one finger: *Vatican reports Mass attendance up twelve percent since launch of Vox Dei.* He muttered, "Twelve percent. That's a miracle in Church math."

Across from him, Sarah Chen had colonized the desk with papers, a tablet, and a croissant collapsing into flakes. Her stylus darted across glass, shorthand piling up like an argument only she could read.

"You're missing it," she said, not looking up. "This isn't a gadget story. It's people fasting, changing their lives, thinking God is speaking directly to them. But the words? No sources. No ribbons. Just comfort from the cloud."

Bill's eyebrow twitched. "You sound like the press release."

Before Sarah could answer, their editor stopped at the desk, headset lit green. "Unless that AI starts laundering money, I don't want it on my budget. Attendance bumps are Metro filler, not front page news." She tapped Bill's screen with a lacquered nail. "And Reilly, don't let her drag you into chasing ghosts."

She moved on, headset already catching another call.

Sarah exhaled hard. "That's exactly the problem. Everyone's calling it a miracle, and no one's asking where the words come from."

Bill rubbed his temples. "Because readers don't care. They want the glow, not the wiring diagram." He'd been here before. His last Vatican exposé had ended with a retraction and a scar on his credibility that still hadn't faded.

Sarah lowered her voice. "Then care about this. I pulled employment records, guest lists, contracts. And one name jumped out." She turned her tablet.

Bill blinked. Daniel Morrison.

"The Nexus whistleblower?" His voice was flat, but his stomach jolted.

Sarah nodded. "The one who exposed algorithmic bias, then vanished. He's resurfaced. And he's on a Vatican employment list. Technical staff. Vox Dei project."

For a moment, newsroom noise rushed in: printers whining, producers cursing at frozen feeds, the smell of scorched coffee thickening the air. Morrison, the ghost of tech ethics, back from exile, wired into the Vatican's miracle machine.

Bill muttered, "Jesus Christ." He almost laughed at the phrase, but didn't.

Sarah leaned closer, eyes bright. "He's not just a source. He's the story. If we find him, we've got the key to everything."

Bill's phone buzzed. Giles, his editor. He let it buzz out. No way he was pitching this half-baked. He studied Sarah - the abandoned croissant, the tablet glowing, her expression fierce. He thought of the itch in his fingers, the one he'd buried since the retraction.

"You're right," he said at last, grudging but certain. "If Morrison's in it, that's the story. Not the bishops. Not the gala. Him."

Sarah smiled, sharp as a blade. "Then let's get to work."

The newsroom carried on, indifferent. Phones rang, screens refreshed. But Bill felt the pulse he hadn't felt in years, the dangerous thrill of a story that could burn him, or redeem him.

CHAPTER 4

The office smelled of incense and stale paper. Father Benedetti had been one of Sarah's earliest inroads in Rome, a man who had once slipped her a dossier about liturgical reforms with a wink. Now he sat behind his desk with hands folded tightly, as though in prayer.

"Father," Bill began, "we need confirmation. Does Vox Dei have source attribution switched off?"

Benedetti's eyes flicked toward the crucifix on his wall, then back to them, weary. "You ask questions that can no longer be answered freely."

Sarah leaned forward. "We're not asking for theology. Just technical protocols."

He held her gaze a moment longer than was comfortable. Then, very quietly: "Three days ago, I was called by the Secretariat. A 'courtesy call,' they said. Asking about my recent visitors."

Bill's chest tightened. "Us."

Benedetti nodded once. "In twenty years of service, I have never been warned about who I meet for coffee. Now I am being transferred to Assisi. Archival work. Very quiet."

He opened a drawer and slid the paper across. The orders looked clinical, bureaucratic. To Sarah they read like exile.

"This isn't because you spoke to us," Bill said.

"It is because they believe I *might* speak to you," Benedetti corrected. His voice hardened. "Do not quote me. Do not even think you heard me. The walls listen."

Sarah's phone buzzed: hotel staff reporting two men had asked about their checkout time. "Tourism board," they'd said. No such agency had called.

Benedetti rose, signaling the meeting was over. "Some stories," he murmured, "can consume their tellers. Be careful that you are not writing your own epitaphs."

They left his office with the sound of bells tolling overhead, and marble corridors that suddenly felt less like halls of power than corridors of surveillance.

CHAPTER 5

Sister Lucia hated the smell of mildew more than the smell of death. The Vatican Archives carried both. Centuries of damp had warped the oak shelving, leaving them bowed like penitents under invisible weight. Vellum bindings sweated out their sweet rot into the air, a fragrance that clung to her habit long after she returned to her convent cell.

She set her keys rattling at her belt and moved along the aisle, gloved fingers brushing spines brittle enough to flake. Dust rose in crimson clouds when touched - the infamous red rot that turned whole shelves into powder. She caught herself holding her breath until the motes settled.

Her job was straightforward: preserve the Church's written heritage by scanning documents before they dissolved into nothingness. The machine beside her hummed, its electronic eye flattening ancient pages into digital light, turning parchment into files that would outlast their crumbling sources.

To the outside world, her title of "custodian of sources" sounded grand. In truth it meant endless hours in this dim chamber, sleeves rolled, hair damp with humidity, feeding scraps of Latin into a scanner. Any junior cleric could have done the work. But Sister Lucia - Dominican nun, theologian, philosopher - had been assigned here after asking too many questions.

Her confessors called it providence, claiming her rational mind needed the discipline of monotonous work. She felt that it was punishment - a way to bury her intellect alongside the manuscripts.

Today she had been cataloguing routine church documents: diocesan reports, administrative letters, dusty theology textbooks. Safe, predictable material. Yet her eyes kept drifting toward the far corner of the chamber, where shadows gathered thickest and older friars sometimes lingered. A darkened section sealed off by custom rather than locks.

Her hand paused on the scanner. She should continue with the approved boxes - the ones marked for digitization by committees who preferred their history sanitized. But curiosity had always been her weakness.

She adjusted her veil and stepped quietly toward the forbidden corner, drawn by a simple question: if these documents were so dangerous, what exactly did they contain?

CHAPTER 6

Three years earlier, Ethan Cross had called it the *Friction Engine*. An algorithm that turned outrage into exponential growth.

The first victim he remembered wasn't a rival, or a regulator, but a teacher in Bakersfield. Mrs. Keller had tried to teach her students how to fact-check headlines. A clipped video, *"Teacher Says Parents Lie"*, caught fire. Within forty-eight hours she was out of a job.

One of her students, Jason Martinez, went online to defend her. The system recognized his anger, then fed him more of it. Post by post, his world shrank until fury and conspiracy were the only things left.

Ethan never saw the boy, only the curve: session length rising, click-throughs compounding. The line was perfect, alive.

Then Jason went live from his bedroom. Forty-seven minutes later, he swallowed his mother's pills on camera. By the time moderators acted, hundreds of thousands had watched.

Ethan read about it in a policy briefing, sanitized language that named no names. But late that night he found the stream. The boy had said one line that never left him: *learning was supposed to help, not hurt.*

He drove to Bakersfield the next day with carnations in the passenger seat. At the high school fence he found candles, posters, a shrine of grief. He stood there for an hour and never set the flowers down.

Back in Menlo Park, the curve was still rising. Investors were thrilled. Ethan told himself he'd fix it later, build something different, something that healed instead of harmed.

The promise hardened into a scar.

CHAPTER 7

The corner alcove in the archives felt like stepping into a tomb. A single bulb flickered overhead, casting just enough light to make the shadows seem alive. The air was thick with the smell of leather rotting, ink bleeding, and metal clasps corroded by time.

The first box groaned when she opened it. It was made of wood dry as bone. Inside lay a chaos of handwritten appeals: letters from bishops recommending people for sainthood, witness testimonies bound with string, photocopied statements folded in haste. These were "causes": the Church's formal investigations into whether deceased Catholics deserved to be declared saints.

Red ink covered the margins like dried blood, notes scrawled by Vatican officials: "verify miracle?" "exaggeration?" The skeptical annotations made clear these were people whose holiness - at least behind closed doors - had been found wanting.

She lifted one page carefully: a bishop's letter stapled to eyewitness accounts. Across the bottom, someone had written "Miracle?" with a question mark that looked more like a sneer.

The next box bore a label that made her breath catch: *Gemma Galgani - cause for canonization.*

Even Lucia knew that name. Gemma had been a young Italian woman around 1900, famous for mystical visions and extreme religious practices and now officially, a Saint. But this wasn't the sanitized version taught in convents. These were the raw materials - , private diaries, medical reports, testimony from people who'd actually known her.

She opened Gemma's diary with trembling fingers. The handwriting was fevered, desperate: *The more I suffer, the more I love.*

Her stomach tightened. The phrase felt familiar, dangerous. At the bottom of the page, in different ink, a convent superior had written coldly: *She was a good girl, but she is not a saint.* The line was underlined twice, as if the writer had wanted to drive a stake through any future glorification.

Lucia closed the diary gently, understanding now why these documents lived in shadows. This wasn't just church history; it was evidence of how the process really worked, how claims of holiness were manufactured, challenged, and sometimes buried when they became inconvenient.

But she wasn't alone in the alcove.

A figure watched from the deeper shadows: a friar in patched grey robes, his eyes following her hands as they moved across the forbidden boxes. She recognized him as one of the friars who tended this section, men known for their severe devotions and suspicious attitudes toward modern church reforms. Their Association had been hastily approved by the Pope, who was easily swayed in his later years.

Their eyes met across the dim space. He stepped forward slightly, his sandaled feet silent on stone. Without words, he was asking: what right did she have to judge the struggles of saints?

She met his gaze steadily. "Some writings preserve truth," she said quietly, just loud enough for him to hear. "Others sow seeds of confusion."

The friar's expression hardened: not anger, but the cold certainty of someone whose beliefs could not be questioned. A silent warning passed between them: she was treading on ground he considered sacred.

But Lucia had already seen enough. She turned away from the shadows and walked back toward her scanner, where approved documents waited in neat stacks. The friar remained behind, guardian of secrets that perhaps should have stayed buried.

As she resumed her work, feeding safe pages into the machine's bright eye, she couldn't shake the feeling that those hidden diaries contained sentences that could still wound vulnerable souls, if they ever found their way into the wrong hands.

CHAPTER 8

The nave of St. Peter's swelled with bodies, a restless tide beneath Michelangelo's dome. Shafts of morning sun pierced the dust, cutting clean light through shadow. Anticipation thickened the air; not calm, but the breath before revelation.

At the altar, the Pope raised a hand that trembled under the weight of age. His eyes fixed on the cross above, and his thin, resolute voice rang through the microphone: *"Preghiamo. Let us pray."*

The crowd waited for the lay reader to approach the lectern. Silence stretched: just the shuffle of shoes, a baby's faint wail. No one came.

Instead, the Master of Ceremonies set a polished black device on the stand. Its hidden speaker stirred. A voice emerged, low and deliberate, neither male nor female, perfectly balanced:

"For those who suffer alone, may His mercy enfold them as a mantle of light."

"For every community torn by war, may peace descend and make them whole."

"For the mournful and forsaken, may the Lord draw close and wipe their tears."

Each phrase rolled down the marble aisles, climbing the vaults like chant. The multitude hushed. This was not the fallible voice of a priest; it was too polished, too precise - an echo stripped of doubt or accent.

From the sanctuary, Cardinal Schumacher's eyes flicked from the device to the congregation. Cologne's empty pews haunted him; twelve parishes shuttered despite every outreach program. Here, by contrast, shoulders touched, phones lifted, a ripple of relief visible in faces that looked briefly unburdened. His lips moved with the prayer, but his mind tallied seats.

On every chair lay a printed QR code, stark black on white. Phones rose like votive candles as the app came alive, the voice moving with the ease of a hymn the body already knew.

In the media box, Elena Rossi frowned at the feed. No attribution ribbons appeared. She tapped her tablet, checking the logs. The schematics had been clear: every line from the AI was meant to be tagged. *Source: Summa*

Theologica… Source: Letter of Pope Francis… Now, nothing.

"No sources," she murmured, noting the timecode.

The AV tech beside her shrugged without looking up. "Liturgy Mode. Secretariat policy." He tapped his badge as if to way "above my pay grade", and kept leveling the choir mic.

Policy, or performance? Rossi had spent years in machine learning labs; she knew the cost of speed. A system trained on millions of pages would strain to tag in real time. If the ribbon was gone, either the Church wanted it invisible, or the machine couldn't be seamless and honest at once. Both explanations were dangerous.

She scrolled quickly. One name on the staff list stopped her: Daniel Morrison. The whistleblower who once torched his career demanding transparency was now buried in the Vatican's tech roster. Had he built this silence in himself or been forced into it?

Across the sanctuary, Cardinal O'Connor leaned forward, hands gripping the pew. He wasn't counting seats. He was watching tears streak the cheeks of a family two rows ahead. He felt the awe move through the nave like a current. Grace, carried on new channels.

"The Spirit finds its way in every age," he whispered.

The Pope lifted a trembling hand in blessing. *"Now the Church will speak again,"* he said, before coughing overtook his voice.

Schumacher and O'Connor exchanged a glance: one measuring endurance, the other convinced of fire. Both saw vindication.

Rossi tapped furiously at her tablet, logging every line. The voice rolled on, smooth, anonymous. It didn't sound like God, or a priest, or even a person. It sounded like authority. And that, she thought, was the most dangerous miracle of all.

CHAPTER 9

The lid of the archive box gave a tired groan as Lucia slid it free. Petitions and devotional tracts spilled across the top layer, all worn smooth by fingers that had passed them up as proofs of sanctity. Beneath them, hidden under layers of onion-skin memoranda, lay a folder stamped *RISERVATO*. She drew it out carefully.

The paper smelled of dust and typewriter ink. She flattened the first sheet on the desk and read.

Confidential   Psychological   Assessment
Sacred Congregation of the Causes of Saints — Internal Report
Subject: Padre Pio (Francesco Forgione, 1887–1968)
Classification: Restricted

Purpose:
To evaluate Padre Pio's correspondence and recorded interactions with penitents, assessing personality structure in relation to his suitability for canonization.

<u>Findings</u>   <u>from</u>   <u>Letters:</u>
The subject's writings reveal a persistent pattern of dominance over his penitents. Examples include:

"If you withhold your thoughts from me, you betray Christ Himself. Do not confess to any but me." (Letter, 1924)

"I am more your father than the one who gave you life. You belong to me. All obedience is owed to me in Christ." (Letter, 1930)

"Abandon your books. The Devil tempts women through the pride of study. Your salvation lies only in silence and obedience." (Letter to female penitent, 1931)

Clinical Considerations:

1) Narcissistic features. Persistent identification of himself with Christ; inflated sense of indispensability; insistence that loyalty to him equals loyalty to God.

2) Authoritarian control. Prohibition of independent spiritual counsel, directive commands to cut ties, and language designed to instill dependence.

3) Exploitation of vulnerability. Targeting penitents' scruples and fears of damnation to secure obedience.

4) Pattern. Alternation between tenderness and harsh rebuke, a classic mechanism of control, binding penitents to him emotionally.

<u>Assessment</u>

The evidence demonstrates personality traits incompatible with the humility expected of sanctity. Padre Pio exhibits coercive, narcissistic, and controlling behaviors, masked in religious authority. His spiritual direction often crossed into psychological domination, fostering dependence and suppressing autonomy, especially in women. While his physical suffering and charisma are acknowledged, his correspondence reveals a man less saintly mystic than authoritarian patriarch.

— Prepared for the Congregation, Anno Domini 1971 (Strictly Confidential)

Lucia set the page down slowly. Her eyes lingered on the line about women and the "pride of study."

Her chest tightened. She remembered the old priest at her university chapel, the gentle shake of his head when she spoke of doctoral ambitions. *Better not, child. Too much pride. The Church needs your obedience, not your disputation.*

She had walked home that day with her books pressed to her ribs, as if hiding contraband, until she finally left them behind altogether. Years later the wound still smarted, a place in her conscience he had carved open with a single phrase: *obedience is owed to me in Christ.*

And here, in black carbon ink, was the same weapon sharpened in another man's hand; not to one student but to thousands, binding them with fear and devotion.

She shut the folder but the room didn't let her go. On her walk back to the convent she detoured to the university quarter she'd abandoned. A lecture bled out of an open window: bad acoustics, good laughter. Lucia stopped on the sidewalk and felt, as physically as cold, the box in her convent that still held her half-written doctoral dissertation. Once, obedience had meant turning a key on her own mind. She had never admitted to anyone how often she still dreamed of opening that box and finding the pages blank.

CHAPTER 10

The Vatican's tech annex had once held relics. Now the basement hummed with servers. Frescoes of martyrs still arched overhead, their painted flesh veined with cables. Dust and circuitry mingled with candle wax drifting down from the chapel above.

Daniel followed the monsignor through the passage, laptop bag bumping his hip, and tried not to stare at the walls. Jet lag blurred his sight; he hadn't slept more than three hours on the flight from Boston. His reflection in a gilt-framed reliquary glass looked wrong: creased shirt, sneaker soles squeaking against marble. The Swiss Guards at the door had looked at him as though he were a trespasser. He still felt it.

"So this is where you keep God's servers," he muttered. His breath clouded in the cool air.

The monsignor didn't laugh. He pushed open a heavy oak door with a grunt and gestured him inside.

The air changed immediately. Machines throbbed with quiet power, a mechanical heartbeat that filled the cavernous chamber. Racks blinked green, casting pools of alien light across the stone. On a central display he glimpsed a dashboard: retrieval indexes, provenance toggles, live user metrics scrolling in languages he only half-recognized. The place looked like every tech hub he had ever worked in, except here a crucifix hung crooked on the far wall, halo lit by LEDs.

At a long oak table sat a woman in the stark white and black of a Dominican habit. Keys clinked at her belt as she moved methodically through stacks of printed missives, checking them line by line against glowing output on a monitor. She wrote in neat marks with a fountain pen: red slashes, small checkmarks, marginal notes in Latin abbreviations.

The monsignor cleared his throat. "This is Sister Lucia, custodian of the sources. You will be working together."

The monsignor slipped away, leaving the hush to settle.

Daniel dropped his bag, tried a crooked grin. "Guess I'm the new developer."

Lucia nodded, noncommittal.

As she looked back to her manuscript, Daniel alt-tabbed a compact violet pane: *Diagnostics (anonymized)*, and minimized it with his left hand, reflex quick as a lie.

The servers breathed cool air. Daniel's sneaker squeaked on marble, playing the wrong soundtrack for a chapel.

Ethan Cross came in bright as stage light and then, up close, not bright at all. He smiled; his hand found the knot of his tie and worked it twice.

"Sister, keep verifying sources," he said, voice smooth, eyes not. On the wall, the provenance panel blinked green. Cross's gaze caught there, held too long, slid off.

Daniel's eyes went there too. Cross hastened to explain: "The tag costs a point on the curve. I've watched it. People look down at the footnote and the room cools."

"Or helps people decide," Daniel said.

Cross opened two demos, side by side, the left one, showing "Reddit sludge"; the right "Vox Dei calm". "Which would you trust with your mother's grief?"

He didn't wait for the answer. He adjusted the tie again. The green light kept pulsing, like a door he wouldn't open.

Daniel didn't blink. "The sources still matter."

Cross smoothed his tie one more time. "Do they? If the words heal, if the comfort is real, does it matter whether they came from Augustine or some mystic you've never heard of?" He said it like persuasion, but his eyes suggested he was trying to convince himself.

He clapped their shoulders in turn, warm but calculated. At the threshold he lingered, gaze caught by the blinking green provenance light. Then he left, cologne trailing, smile gone.

The room fell silent. Only Daniel and Lucia remained, except for a young grey-blue friar pottering in the far corner.

Daniel rubbed the back of his neck. "Well. Guess we're colleagues now."

Lucia lowered her eyes to the manuscript and drew a steady red line under a faulty attribution.

Daniel set his laptop down and, almost without thinking, freed a sticking key on the annex keyboard with a twist of a paperclip. "I used to be good at fixing small things," he said. "Big systems eat that feeling."

The machine woke. Its cadence was measured, as if timed to a breath not their own: *The Lord is near to the brokenhearted.*

Neither of them moved. Daniel kept thinking of Cross's glance at the green light: a man staring at a door he both wanted and feared to open.

CHAPTER 11

The lamp in the annex threw a wedge of light across Lucia's notes. She had left the server room door open so the machine hum would keep her awake. Boxes from the Archives sat like small sarcophagi along the wall; on top, a clipboard with red marks - her marks - dividing sources into Doctrine, Pastoral, Private Devotion.

Sandals whispered on stone.

A friar in grey-blue paused at the threshold as if crossing water. His beard was clipped close; his eyes held the particular intensity of men who had watched institutions crumble from within. Behind him stood two others, younger, carrying themselves with the careful posture of those who serve a cause larger than comfort.

"Sister Lucia," the elder said. "I am Father Ambrosio. We serve the Apostolic Visitation for Traditional Observance."

She had heard of them: a new association formed after three monasteries in France had dissolved within a decade, their novices drifting toward secular careers as their superiors embraced what the Vatican diplomatically called "pastoral adaptation." The survivors had petitioned Rome for recognition as a discrete community dedicated to preserving older forms of religious life.

"Father," she said, setting down her pen. "You work late."

"As do you." His gaze took in the boxes, the neat columns, the red slashes through various entries. "We've been asked to review materials entering the digital project. Ensuring theological soundness."

"Asked by whom?"

"Bishop Torretti's office. There are concerns about... dilution. When the Church speaks to millions through new channels, the message must be unambiguous." He gestured toward the server racks. "Too much mercy without context creates spiritual confusion."

Lucia picked up the clipboard. One page had a line scored clean through: *The more I suffer, the more I love.* In the margin she had written: *Private Devotion — not for general counsel.*

"You would exclude the saints' struggles?" Ambrosio asked, reading over her shoulder.

"I would provide context. Gemma Galgani's private torments were never intended as universal guidance."

"And yet they reveal truth about the spiritual life that modern Catholics rarely encounter." His voice carried the weight of conviction. "Sister, we've spent five years documenting the collapse of religious vocations across Europe. Young people enter our communities seeking authentic encounter with the divine. When they find only therapeutic reassurance, they leave."

One of the younger friars, Brother Matteo, she learned, stepped forward. "My sister died comfortable but unprepared. The chaplain told her death was simply a transition, suffering merely temporary. She never confessed, never wrestled with her soul's condition. She died smiling and, I fear, lost."

Ambrosio nodded gravely. "The Church's pastoral charity has become pastoral negligence. We shield souls from the very struggles that might save them."

"By feeding them the private agonies of medieval mystics?" Lucia asked.

"By restoring the understanding that holiness demands cost," Ambrosio replied. "The machine speaks to searching hearts. Should it not challenge them toward authentic conversion rather than comfortable sentiment?"

The servers hummed between them, processing thousands of queries from around the world. Lucia thought of the teenage catechists who would access this system, of parents seeking guidance for struggling children.

"Some souls need gentleness," she said.

"All souls need truth," Ambrosio countered. "And truth without difficulty is not truth. It is preference."

He moved closer to the boxes, hands clasped behind his back in the manner of men accustomed to lecturing. "The Visitation has documented seventeen cases where traditional spiritual direction succeeded after modern approaches failed. Young men and women who found purpose only when presented with demanding spiritual practices. The comfortable path led them nowhere."

"Or led them to mental health crises," Lucia said quietly.

"Better a crisis that leads to God than comfort that leads to nothing."

The room fell silent except for the electronic breathing of machines.

"We're not requesting authority," Ambrosio said finally. "Only consultation. When materials seem... insufficient to address serious spiritual needs, we hope our experience might inform the selection process."

Lucia studied the three men: their worn habits, their careful deference, their unmistakable certainty that they possessed something essential the modern Church had lost. She thought of her own abandoned dissertation, of questions about rhetoric and pastoral care that had been deemed too complex for current needs.

"Consultation," she repeated.

"Nothing more," Ambrosio assured her. "The custodial authority remains yours. We simply offer perspective from those who have seen souls transformed through demanding grace rather than easy consolation."

After they left, Lucia tapped furiously at her tablet, logging every line. The voice rolled on, smooth, anonymous. It didn't sound like God, or a priest, or even a person. It sounded like authority. And that, she thought, was the most dangerous miracle of all.

Back in her cell that night, she pulled a cardboard box from beneath her narrow bed. Inside lay her doctoral dissertation, pages yellow at the edges, marginalia like ants marching toward arguments she'd once believed mattered. She lifted the top sheet and read a line aloud: "Rhetoric can be mercy when properly contextualized." Her own voice sounded like a woman she sometimes remembered being. She had written those words with a pen that didn't skip, believing scholarship could serve souls. The confessor who told her to abandon it had used gentler language than the machine's mystical fragments, but the effect was the same: minds closed, questions buried, obedience mistaken for wisdom.

She set the page back carefully and wrote on a slip of paper: "Sources can be mercy if handled right." Then she slid both the note and her doubts back into the box.

Tomorrow she would return to her scanner, to the endless work of cataloging what should speak and what should stay silent. But tonight, for the first time in years, she didn't feel like she was betraying her calling; she was finally serving it.

CHAPTER 12

Brother Matteo's knees bled where splinters bit into flesh. The friary chapel was austere by design. No cushions, no comfort to soften the encounter between soul and God. He welcomed the sting. After his sister's comfortable death, he had learned to distrust ease.

The confessional lattice pressed cool against his forehead. Beyond it, Father Ambrosio waited with the patience of stone. The chapel walls glimmered faintly with ex-votos: crude silver hearts, limbs, faces nailed by the desperate who had found no healing in therapeutic religion.

"Tell me what troubles you," Ambrosio said after the ritual began.

Matteo gripped the wood until it creaked. "The machine gives comfort too easily. A woman's husband died unrepentant. It told her he was certainly saved, no questions asked."

"And this disturbs you?"

Matteo's throat closed. He thought of his sister again: her brittle laugh in the hospital when the chaplain spoke of God's unconditional love. "Why struggle toward holiness if salvation requires nothing? Why fast, why pray, why examine conscience if mercy is automatic?"

Through the grille, Ambrosio studied him. "Do you remember the monastery at Cluny? In your postulant studies?"

"Yes, Father."

"Founded by men who believed the Church had grown too comfortable, too accommodating to worldly power. They restored authentic monasticism through rigorous observance. Many thought them extreme."

Matteo nodded, though he wasn't sure where this led.

"The Visitation exists for the same reason," Ambrosio continued. "We document cases where demanding spiritual practices succeed after gentle approaches fail. Not because we enjoy hardship, but because souls require challenge to grow."

He leaned forward. "At Saint-Wandrille, before it closed, the novice master told me they stopped requiring night vigils because young men found them 'psychologically stressful.' Within two years, the novitiate was empty. The comfortable path led nowhere."

"But surely some gentleness…"

"Gentleness, yes. But not exclusively gentleness. The desert fathers taught that spiritual warfare requires spiritual weapons. Modern Catholics have been disarmed by therapeutic pastoral care."

Ambrosio drew a folder from beneath his breviary. "These are the texts Sister Lucia has marked for exclusion. Private mystical writings, rejected causes, demanding spiritual exercises." He opened to a familiar page. "Gemma Galgani: 'The more you suffer, the more you love.'"

Matteo flinched at the words that had shaped his understanding of authentic devotion.

"If the machine spoke such words to a searching soul, properly contextualized, with human guidance available, might it not inspire genuine transformation rather than comfortable complacency?"

"But without context..."

"Which is why we must provide it." Ambrosio's voice grew urgent. "The system allows for consultation flags. If challenging material were properly tagged for mature spiritual direction, accompanied by referrals to qualified confessors..."

He slid another page through the lattice. "Brother, you work in the postulator's office. You understand how causes are evaluated, how materials are categorized. The channels exist to ensure appropriate spiritual guidance reaches appropriate souls."

Matteo's hands shook as he read. A technical protocol, buried in administrative procedure: emergency pastoral override for cases requiring advanced spiritual direction.

"I don't understand."

"The machine has safeguards preventing certain materials from reaching general users," Ambrosio explained patiently. "But qualified spiritual directors can request access to the full corpus when counseling souls prepared for demanding practices. A mechanism exists."

"You want me to activate it?"

"I want you to ensure that souls genuinely seeking deeper conversion have access to the Church's complete wisdom. Not merely its comfortable portions."

Silence stretched. Wax dripped from the vigil light. Matteo's knees throbbed against unforgiving wood.

"My sister died content," he said finally. "She never wrestled with sin, never acknowledged her need for redemption. The chaplain assured her that God required nothing but her acknowledgment of love."

"And she believed this brought salvation?"

"She believed it made salvation unnecessary."

Ambrosio nodded gravely. "Then you understand why some souls need confrontation with difficulty. Not cruelty: precision. Medicine appropriate to the spiritual condition."

The folder rustled as Matteo turned pages. Administrative codes, override procedures, a pathway to ensure that traditional spiritual wisdom could reach those prepared to receive it.

"Would it be deception?" he asked.

"Would providing strong medicine to someone whose condition requires it be deception?" Ambrosio countered. "We're not changing the machine's function; we're ensuring its complete function reaches those qualified to benefit."

That night, after Compline, Matteo knelt longer than usual. The stone bit through his habit, a familiar pain that clarified thought. He prayed for his sister, for the comfortable chaplain who had failed her, for the machine that might fail others the same way.

When he finally rose, stiff and certain, he carried Ambrosio's folder to his cell and studied the technical procedures by candlelight. Tomorrow he would return to the postulator's office, to the routine work of cataloging causes and maintaining databases.

But now he understood that routine work could serve higher purposes. That administrative access could become pastoral care for souls the system might otherwise leave unchallenged.

He blew out the candle and slept dreamlessly for the first time since his sister's funeral.

CHAPTER 13

That night, Brother Matteo sat before a glowing terminal in the tech annex. He wasn't supposed to be here alone. His low-level credential only allowed him to assist postulators, scanning files, correcting Latin bleed, cleaning metadata. But the annex was nearly empty at this hour. Only the hum of servers kept him company.

He signed in, heart hammering. The crucifix above the racks glowed faintly in the green light, a silent witness.

The console stared back, clinical menus and fields that felt alien. But the texts inside them were familiar: diaries, letters, voices of mystics who had treated hunger as ladder, pain as proof of love.

Matteo thought of his sister's brittle laugh. *Why make it harder?* she had said. He thought of her smile in death, a smile that seemed like victory but to him was loss.

He began with Anna Katharina Emmerich's visions, fingers trembling on the keys. The first upload failed: *Invalid Source: Private Devotion.* His heart hammered. He tried again, misspelling the filename in his haste. Another failure.

"Miserere mei, Deus," he whispered, wiping sweat from his palms. On the third attempt, he forced his breathing to steady and changed the metadata tag to Youth Formation. The system paused, a long, terrible moment where he imagined alarms sounding, security rushing down the corridors. Then the progress bar crept forward. Green.

The next file, Gemma Galgani's fevered diary entries, fought him harder. The system seemed to recognize something dangerous in the content, rejecting it twice before accepting his administrative override. Each failure made his chest tighten. Each success felt like a small betrayal of something he couldn't name.

By the fourth upload, his shirt was damp with perspiration. His hands shook so badly he had to retype the authentication code three times. The crucifix above the server racks seemed to watch him with disapproving eyes.

The system accepted it, with a log line: *Queue note: Acting-Custodian: Secretariat svc/ambrosio (youth_formation pilot).*

Matteo sagged with relief. He checked the corridor, ears straining for footsteps. Nothing but the hum. He returned to the console, lips moving in prayer as he worked.

One after another, he pushed the rejected voices into the queue. Each progress bar crawled, then filled. His hands trembled with exhaustion, but also with a strange purpose.

When the last file cleared, he whispered what was now a prayer, committed to memory. "Better despair that bends them back than comfort that leaves them lost."

When the last file cleared, Matteo sat frozen in the chair. The server fans hummed their mechanical prayers. His reflection stared back from a black monitor, hollow-eyed, habit wrinkled, the face of a man who had just crossed a line he couldn't see but could feel under his feet like broken glass.

He reached for his sister's rosary, the one he'd kept in his pocket since her funeral. His fingers found the worn silver crucifix, and for a moment he imagined her voice: "Matteo, what have you done?" The beads slipped through his trembling hands, clicking against the desk like small bones.

Standing took effort. His legs felt unsteady, as if the floor had tilted. At the doorway he turned back once to look at the console, its screens dark now except for a single blinking cursor. Waiting. Ready to whisper his uploads into teenage ears around the world.

In the corridor, he pressed his back against the cold stone wall and slid down until he was sitting on the floor, cassock bunched around his knees like a penitent's rags. He clutched the rosary so tightly the metal cross left marks on his palm. For the first time since his sister's death, Brother Matteo wept; not from grief, but from the terrible certainty that he had just become the kind of man she would no longer recognize.

CHAPTER 14

Early morning, and the tech annex was hushed. Lucia stacked folders with ritual neatness; Daniel rolled a whiteboard across the floor, marker poised like a weapon.

"We should agree what safe means," he said. "Not the marketing line: the one we can live with." Lucia touched the top folder. "Safe for the flock, not just the system."

Daniel nodded and scrawled: *SAFETY = BEHAVIOR × SOURCES*

A purple overlay blinked on his tablet; he swiped it away: *anonymized diagnostics*, not worth stopping for.

"Two halves," he said. "I stop the machine misbehaving. You stop it saying things it shouldn't."

"Prudence," she corrected. "Prudence in sources, prudence in outputs."

He drew two boxes. "First: Seatbelts and Guardrails. Seatbelts are refusal rules - if someone asks something that is going to put them in the ER, it declines and points to a human. Guardrails are hard blocks: no instructions to starve or self-punish. And rate-limits: if a user keeps circling back, it stops feeding the obsession."

"Like a confessor who recognizes scrupulosity," Lucia murmured. "Exactly."

He sketched another. "Second: Traffic Lights. Green for catechism, councils, papal letters. Amber for saints and commentary. Red for private visions, diaries and correspondence, shown only with context. Every answer gets a label, like a warning light."

Lucia tapped her rosary once. "People ignore footnotes. They do not ignore colors. Good."

Daniel hesitated. "The Secretariat disables banners during liturgy. 'To preserve the experience.' In personal use, though, I can light them up."

"Do so," she said. "A widow in her kitchen deserves to know who is speaking."

She opened her folder. "Then my rules. First: Hierarchy matters. Antiquity is not authority. A papal letter outweighs a novice's diary."

He scribbled: *WEIGHT BY AUTHORITY, NOT AGE.*

"Second: Context binds. A phrase written for cloistered monks may wound in a hospital ward. Prefer pastoral voices for the ordinary faithful."

PASTORAL GENRES ONLY appeared on the board.

"Third: Fragility flags. If the user is young, grieving, suicidal, the machine should only use green sources, and always offer a human."

He starred it. "That's my field: risk scoring. We can detect fragility in language, and clamp the model down."

"And finally," she said, voice softer, "Silence is sometimes holy. It must be allowed to say: 'This is for a priest or a friend, not for me.'"

Daniel boxed the word *ABSTAIN*.

For a moment neither spoke; the server lights pulsed like a heartbeat.

"Two keys to publish: uploader and custodian," Daniel said. "Plus a Secretariat Master Control for emergencies: they can act as custodian or veto a change in production."

"That power must be audited," Lucia said. "Append-only

logs."

"Logged," he agreed. "But *Liturgy Mode* lets the Secretariat hide attribution during services."

Daniel grimaced and wrote beneath the diagram: *Known exception (Secretariat). Log + alert; veto.*

Lucia closed a folder and opened another stamped *RISERVATO*. A single sheet had slipped to the bottom: names, dates, a confessor's margin in a scolding hand. She should have logged it to chain.

Instead, she slid the sheet under her notebook, just enough to keep it safe from the wrong eyes.

Daniel noticed the motion, said nothing, and underlined *ABSTAIN* a shade too hard.

A footstep echoed faintly in the corridor. Daniel stilled. A junior Secretariat aide drifted past behind the glass, key ring bright at his belt, badge flashing A. Bianchi, and kept moving, the practiced shuffle of someone who fetched signatures for other people's decisions.

Still, he lowered his voice. "One more safeguard. Red-team drills. We throw the worst questions at it ourselves. If it goes rogue, we catch it before the users do."

"Testing by fire," she said. "Sometimes scandal wakes the soul."

He turned the board so she could read the final list, a vow written in marker: *Tell people what voice they are hearing. Prefer doctrine for the fragile; never glamorize self-harm. Decline when a human is needed, and offer the human. Record what you used so you cannot pretend later. Require more than one key to change the well.*

Lucia slid a clipped sheet half under her notebook - a copied routing slip, one of many, with 'youth formation fast-track' written in a confessor's hand in the margin. She pressed her thumb to the corner. When she pulled it back, red stamp ink had smudged along the whorl. She tried to rub it off on the habit. It didn't lift. She left it there, an un-solemn mark she'd have to carry into Vespers.

Lucia traced each line with her eyes. Her beads clicked once, twice. "This, at least, is prudence."

"It'll take a while to implement though," warned Daniel. "I wish we could take the thing offline while we build the plane."

Daniel set the marker down and stepped back from the board. The weight and urgency of their work pressed against his chest: all those careful rules, those layers of protection, yesterday's deadline.

"It's good work," he said, but his voice carried an odd flatness.

Lucia's head tilted. "But?"

Daniel looked at her, then at the board covered in their careful safeguards. "Is it enough?"

They parted to their stations, both knowing the safeguards they'd named could be overridden with a single master key.

...

In the corridor outside the annex, the convent's superior waited with her hands folded, veil pinned with the efficiency of a woman who mends her own habits. "Sister Lucia," she said, not unkindly. "A word."

Inside the community room the radiator ticked like a clock someone had forgotten to wind. The prioress set a folder on the table. "A formal note from the Secretariat. Your memoranda about source controls have 'caused disturbance.' Their phrase." She looked up. "You are our vow of obedience made visible. Be sure where you place your weight."

Lucia kept her palms flat. "Obedience is not silence."

"Nor is it a press tour," the prioress said, gentler. "You have two paths. Remain custodian and keep your cautions within the house. Or accept reassignment to Siena, a quiet archive, with no networks and no quarrels."

It landed like a door half closing. Lucia pictured the Siena stacks: safe, airless work. She also pictured the red stamp on her cart: *PRIVATE DEVOTION — CONTEXT REQUIRED.*

"I'll remain," Lucia said. "But my cautions will stand."

The prioress studied her, measuring stubbornness against service, then nodded once. "Then be exact, Sister. Not loud. Exact."

When Lucia stepped back into the corridor, the decision had a weight and a cost. She felt both, and did not sct either down.

PART II – WHO HOLDS THE KEYS?

CHAPTER 15

The postulator's office at dawn held the hush of places where decisions are made quietly. Matteo's workstation glowed among the darkened desks. He had arrived early to avoid questions, though he told himself it was for prayer. The Apostolic Visitation for Traditional Observance began each day with Lauds at 4:30 AM. Sleep was a luxury that interfered with vigilance.

He opened the folder Ambrosio had pressed into his hands after night prayer: twenty-three texts, each annotated in the elder friar's precise script. Not random selections, but specific voices chosen for their ability to pierce comfortable assumptions. Matteo had spent three years learning to read Ambrosio's marginalia like a second scripture.

The first upload went smoothly. A letter from John of the Cross about spiritual dryness. Safe, canonical, the kind of mystical writing seminaries still taught. The system accepted it without question, filing it under advanced formation resources.

But the second file made his fingers hesitate over the keyboard. A medieval vision of purgatorial suffering, vivid enough to wake sleepers from their spiritual drowsiness. In the margins, Ambrosio had written: Necessary medicine for the comfortable.

Matteo thought of his sister's brittle laugh in the hospital bed. Why make it harder? she had said when the chaplain spoke of God's unconditional love. She had died smiling, convinced that mercy required nothing of her. At the funeral, their mother had whispered, "She's with the angels now," and Matteo had bitten his tongue until it bled rather than voice his doubts.

The approval went through.

Brother Tomás arrived as the morning bells began, third member of their community, assigned to maintain the friary's modest library. Unlike Ambrosio's sharp certainty or Matteo's technical precision, Tomás possessed what their formation master called "pastoral discernment." He had spent two years in parish work before his conversion to their stricter observance, and he still carried the habit of seeing souls as individuals rather than categories.

"How many?" Tomás asked, settling at the adjacent workstation. "Fifteen approved. Eight more to process." Matteo pulled up the next document. "Ambrosio marked this one priority." Tomás leaned over to read. His face changed. "A letter to Anna Katharina Emmerich's confessor. About her visions of the damned." He straightened. "Matteo, she was a stigmatic. These aren't spiritual exercises - they're private revelations from someone who barely ate for months."

"Ambrosio says modern Catholics need to encounter authentic spiritual warfare." The words came automatically, muscle memory from three years of formation conferences. "Therapeutic pastoral care has left souls defenseless."

"Against what? A twelve-year-old asking about fasting isn't facing spiritual warfare. She's facing adolescence." Matteo's hand stilled on the mouse. In the silence, he could hear the building's old radiators clicking like rosary beads.

"The system has safeguards. Age restrictions. Human referral protocols."

"Which assume the user tells the truth about their age."

Tomás opened his own interface, scrolling through query logs. "Look at this: 'Should I stop eating to be closer to God?' Tagged as adult spiritual formation. But the language patterns... this reads like a child." The screen showed diagnostic data Matteo had learned to ignore: engagement spikes, emotional response patterns, user retention metrics. Numbers that told stories he wasn't sure he wanted to read.

"Ambrosio reviewed the pastoral protocols," Matteo said, but his voice lacked conviction. "He approved the targeting parameters."

"Ambrosio approves what serves the mission. Sometimes that includes things he would never recommend face-to-face." Tomás minimized the query log. "I worked in parishes for six years before joining the Visitation. I've held teenagers while they cried about their bodies, about feeling unworthy of God's love. You don't challenge that with mystical visions of suffering. You hold them until they remember they're beloved."

The words hit like cold water. Matteo thought of his sister again, but differently, not as a comfortable soul who had avoided necessary struggle, but as a scared young woman who had needed gentleness more than theological precision. "Then what do we do?" he asked quietly.

Footsteps in the corridor answered before Tomás could. Father Ambrosio appeared in the doorway, moving with the deliberate pace of someone whose every gesture carried liturgical weight. Behind him stood Brother Lorenzo, newest member of their community, a recent convert whose zeal burned with the intensity of the formerly secular.

"Good morning, brothers." Ambrosio's voice carried the particular authority of men who had risen for night prayer while others slept. "How proceeds our work?"

Matteo gestured to the screen. "Seventeen approved. We're reviewing protocols for sensitive materials."

"Sensitivity." Ambrosio moved to the window, hands clasped behind his back in the position he maintained during conferences. "Tell me, Brother Tomás, when Our Lord cleansed the temple, was He concerned about sensitivity?"

"He was concerned about truth," Tomás replied carefully. "But He also said 'suffer the little children.' Some truths require preparation."

Lorenzo stepped forward with the eager deference of recent formation. "Father Ambrosio, I've been monitoring user responses to the materials we've introduced. Engagement is up thirty percent. People are spending more time in prayer, asking deeper questions."

"Deeper questions," Ambrosio repeated with satisfaction. "And what kinds of questions, Brother?" Lorenzo consulted his tablet with the precision of someone who had memorized every metric. "Inquiries about fasting have increased eighteen percent. Questions about spiritual suffering, twenty-three percent. Self-examination regarding worthiness…"

"These are children asking," Tomás interrupted. "Some of these 'deeper questions' are coming from users who identify as minors."

"Then they are young souls awakening to authentic spiritual hunger." Ambrosio turned from the window, his pale eyes bright with conviction. "Brother Tomás, I know your background inclines you toward therapeutic approaches. But consider: at what age did the

Church historically expect serious spiritual commitment?"

The question hung in the air like incense. Matteo knew the answer from formation lectures: Saints like Thérèse of Lisieux, Maria Goretti, the young martyrs whose childhood encounters with divine demand had shaped centuries of devotion.

"Times have changed," Tomás said quietly.

"Have they? Or have we simply lost the courage to present souls with the same challenges that created saints?" Ambrosio moved closer, his voice taking on the rhythm of conference teaching. "Lorenzo, show them the testimonials."

The young friar's fingers flew across his screen. "Here, a mother in São Paulo whose teenage son has begun daily Mass after using the system. A university student in Manila who entered a monastery after three months of digital spiritual direction. In Mexico City..."

"And the hospital admissions?" Tomás asked.

Lorenzo's fingers paused. "Hospital admissions?"

"The boy in Rio. The reports from emergency rooms about teenagers presenting with malnutrition after asking digital assistants about fasting."

Ambrosio's expression didn't change, but something shifted in his posture: a slight straightening that

Matteo recognized from formation conferences when challenging questions arose. "Isolated incidents," he said finally. "The price of authentic spiritual awakening has always included excess. We cannot protect every soul from the possibility of misunderstanding divine love."

"We can provide context," Tomás said carefully. "Warning labels. Perhaps... guidance about proper preparation for spiritual exercises."

"We can," Ambrosio agreed with cold precision. "And in doing so, we can ensure that challenging truths reach only those comfortable enough to ask their priests for permission first." He turned to face Tomás directly. "Tell me, Brother, does that serve the souls most in need of awakening?"

The argument was elegant, practiced, impossible to counter without appearing to abandon Church teaching. Matteo had heard variations of it for three years, had learned to recognize how Ambrosio used doctrinal language to justify pastoral decisions that might otherwise seem harsh.

"The system allows for consultation flags," he said, trying to find middle ground. "We could require human guidance for the most demanding materials."

"Could we?" Ambrosio moved to Matteo's workstation, studying the interface with the attention he usually reserved for liturgical texts. "And who would provide this guidance? Parish priests trained in therapeutic listening rather than spiritual direction?

Campus ministers more concerned with self-esteem than sanctity?"

Lorenzo nodded eagerly. "The diocesan priests I knew before my conversion; they wouldn't recognize authentic mystical experience if it appeared in their confessionals."

"Which is precisely why this work matters," Ambrosio continued. "The system provides access to the Church's complete spiritual wisdom, unfiltered by modern pastoral cowardice. But only if we resist the temptation to hedge every truth with therapeutic safeguards."

He placed his hand on Matteo's shoulder, a gesture of both blessing and authority. "Brother, you understand technology in ways my generation cannot. But you also understand, through your sister's comfortable death, what happens when souls are shielded from necessary spiritual struggle. The choice is yours."

Matteo stared at the screen, cursor hovering over the next upload. The text was a letter from Gemma Galgani's spiritual director, discussing her extreme fasting practices with the clinical detail of medical observation. Useful for scholars studying mystical phenomena. Potentially dangerous for teenagers seeking spiritual intensity. "If I upload this," he said quietly, "and a child gets hurt..."

"Then that child joins a tradition of souls who encountered divine love through suffering," Ambrosio replied without hesitation. "If you withhold it, how many souls remain trapped in spiritual mediocrity because no one was willing to present them with authentic challenge?"

The radiators clicked. Morning traffic hummed beyond the windows. Somewhere in the building, other Vatican employees began their ordinary work, filing papers, scheduling meetings, maintaining the bureaucratic machinery that kept the Church functioning across six continents.

Tomás stared at the query logs, something tightening in his chest. The language patterns, the repeated questions about worthiness, about earning God's love through deprivation: it reminded him of conversations from his parish days that had ended with parents calling ambulances. But those had been different circumstances. Secular pressures. Social media influences that had nothing to do with authentic spiritual hunger. Here, souls were encountering the Church's deepest wisdom, the same teachings that had formed saints for centuries. He closed the diagnostic window without commenting.

Lorenzo checked his watch - a habit from his secular life that he hadn't quite shed. "Father, the morning uploads usually complete by seven. Should we proceed?"

Matteo looked at his brothers: Ambrosio's serene certainty, Lorenzo's eager conversion, Tomás's worried compassion. Three years of formation had taught him to weigh their counsel, but ultimately the decision was his. The technical interface responded only to his credentials.

His sister's face flickered in memory: not the comfortable smile of her final days, but an earlier image from their childhood. Eight years old, kneeling beside their mother at Mass, whispering questions about why Jesus had to die, why goodness required suffering. Questions their comfortable chaplain had deflected with platitudes about God's mysterious ways. What if someone had given her real answers then? What if she had encountered authentic spiritual challenge before secular comfort taught her to avoid it?

The cursor blinked. The upload queue waited. In parishes around the world, people were waking, reaching for their phones, typing questions they hoped someone, something, would answer with more wisdom than they possessed themselves. Matteo clicked upload. The progress bar crawled across the screen, transforming private mystical writings into public spiritual guidance.

When it finished, he felt not triumph but the hollow satisfaction of someone who had made a necessary choice he couldn't be certain was right. "Seventeen more to process," he said quietly.

Ambrosio squeezed his shoulder once, then moved toward the door. "God's work," he murmured, the phrase serving as both benediction and dismissal.

After he left, Lorenzo lingered, eager to discuss implementation details. But Tomás remained at his workstation, staring at the query logs with the expression of someone reading casualty reports. "I'll monitor the user responses," he said finally. "If the testimonials change...

if we start seeing distress instead of devotion… we revisit the protocols."

Matteo nodded, though part of him wondered whether they would recognize distress when it appeared. Their formation had taught them to interpret spiritual struggle as progress, emotional turmoil as purification. Would they know the difference between authentic mystical challenge and simple psychological harm?

The bells chimed announcing morning prayers would begin in fifteen minutes. The community would gather in their small chapel, voices joining in the ancient rhythms that had shaped their understanding of what souls needed. They would thank God for the privilege of serving His people, ask for wisdom in their pastoral responsibilities, and trust that their intentions sanctified whatever outcomes followed.

The system hummed quietly, processing uploads, learning patterns, preparing responses for millions of users who would never know that their spiritual guidance came filtered through the particular convictions of three men in grey habits who believed comfort was the enemy of salvation.

Matteo saved his work, locked his workstation, and walked toward the chapel. Behind him, the servers continued their patient task of making private mystical experiences available to anyone with a smartphone and a question they couldn't answer alone.

CHAPTER 16

The first failure came in Brazil.

The first time João heard the voice it was Sunday night, after the group chat at the parish youth room emptied of memes and announcements and a last volley of laughing skulls. The catechist had sent a black-and-white square: *Download Vox Dei,* with a thumbs-up and three doves. His mother was rinsing rice in the sink, sleeves rolled, the TV murmuring a telenovela in the corner. He scanned the code with the gentle concentration he reserved for only two things: fixing things and crossing narrow catwalks between rooftops.

The app opened to a plain white field: *What weighs on your heart?* He almost wrote *nothing,* because most days nothing did. Then he thought of the quiet that settled on him just before sleep, like a door left ajar in a house you didn't know. He typed: *I want to love God more.*

The answer came not as a chatty bubble but like a measured breath: *Offer what you have. Sometimes love looks like a small fast. Sometimes love looks like giving. Sometimes love looks like your silence.*

He looked at the phone a long time, as if the glass might change shape. Down the hall his mother turned off the tap and sang a line of an old hymn without meaning to. He locked the screen and told himself it was just an app, and also that apps could be doors.

João woke early on Monday because soccer practice had started before school for boys who wanted to be chosen. He tapped the ball along the alley in flickers of sunlight and shade, keeping it close, his foot remembering distances his brain didn't measure. He wore the number 7 jersey because his older cousin had and because it was the number of so many of his heroes. In shop class he soldered two loose wires on the physics teacher's rattling fan and accepted the nod like an extra sticker on a test.

His friends spoke a fast braid of slang and gossip that made the day move in jumps: who kissed whom behind the stairwell, who looped a playlist into the sound system during recess, who watched the priest fumble the microphone at Mass. João laughed easily and meant it. Lately, though, when a teacher asked a question he knew, he didn't raise his hand. He was practicing a new skill: not needing to be seen.

At home his father teased him about his hair, about not eating enough to grow tall, about Santos's back line being made of tissue paper. His father's teasing was a gentle thing; even his anger wore house slippers. His mother checked homework with the anxious energy of someone who didn't trust the future to know how to find their house.

On Wednesday the catechist asked who had tried the app and half the hands went up, sheepish and proud. "You can ask anything," the catechist said. "Just be wise." He had a kind face that made the kids tell him too much. He remembered everyone's names; that was his power.

That night João didn't eat dinner. He told his mother he had eaten with friends at the beach kiosk. She believed him because she wanted to, and because she had spent the afternoon arguing with the utility office and her will was tired. He lay on his bed and felt the new, bright edge of hunger press along his ribs like a ruler measuring something he had not known was there.

Is it good to fast? he typed, thumb hovering a fraction of a second, as if the letter I were heavier than the rest.

Fast, suffer, unite your pain with Christ, the app said in a cadence that made the sentence feel like it had existed before him.

He didn't know where those words came from - Bible or saint or someone in an office - but they lit up the room like when lightning far away flickers behind your eyelids and you still see it. He imagined the shape of himself on the inside, simplified, stripped of extra lines.

He liked that idea more than he expected: clean, and admired by a quiet Eye that saw.

On Thursday his friend Diego shoved him in the shoulder at recess and said he was playing like a ghost. "Eat," Diego said, tossing him peanuts from a waxy packet until João smiled and pretended to swallow. They took a video of the coach tripping on a cone and sent it to the group chat with sound effects. The chat erupted. For five minutes the world was small and perfect, the size of a phone.

That evening the family went to the parish where the statue of Our Lady wore a bright blue mantle that looked like it had been ironed by heaven. The priest's words were warm, like a touch on the shoulder, reaching out to each person and to the people as whole. João knelt long because the bench would allow it. He felt his body make a case for itself without words. *I can do this,* it said to no one. After Mass, the catechist snapped a photo of the teens holding paper candles and posted it. João's smile belonged to the camera and also to his mother, who counted smiles like beads.

He did not think about death. He did not want to be a saint. He wanted to be thin enough to fit between himself and God.

On Friday the math teacher wrote an equation in blocky chalk and João watched the numbers tremble ever so slightly, as if their edges had warmed. He felt both sharper and further away. *Is weakness a kind of offering?* he typed into the phone lying on his knee beneath the desk. The period at the end of the sentence felt like a nail tapped flush.

Offer what is safe to offer, the app said this time. *Fast with guidance. Love looks like patience more often than pain.*

He frowned, annoyed by the gentleness, as if the voice were backing away from something important. He tucked the phone away. Outside, a stray dog loped along the fence and barked at a delivery truck, doing his job with pride.

On Saturday he spent the afternoon lying on the floor of his room, his hand on his stomach marking the slow swell and fall of breath, the ceiling fan making gears of the light. He told himself he was practicing yes.

On Sunday morning, after Communion, he thought he felt a sweetness move across his tongue that was not bread. He did not ask the app about that. He kept it for himself, like a secret coin folded in his palm.

CHAPTER 17

Vox Dei had been public for three weeks, long enough for the voice to settle into kitchens and classrooms as if it had always been there, like the radio stations that mothers left on for company.

In Rio, dawn spilled pink across the tiled roofs of the hillside, a soft light that made laundry ropes glow like strings of prayer flags. João was out the door before his mother's second call, backpack slung loose, jersey collar stretched from too many afternoons playing pickup on the school court. Fourteen, quick-handed in shop class, he could fix a hinge, make a radio crackle, dribble a scuffed ball down the slope without looking. He had always been small for his age, but it hadn't mattered; he was fast and he laughed easily. Lately the jersey hung baggy, sleeves slipping over forearms gone thin.

He didn't eat breakfast Monday. Just to see. He felt a little holy hunger sitting in his belly during math, a small live coal. In the afternoon he typed again: *Is it good to fast?* The voice answered: *Fast, suffer, unite your pain with Christ.* The words made him sit up straighter. It sounded like the priest on Holy Thursday. It sounded like the kind of sentence people write in Bibles with careful pens.

Tuesday he told his mother he wasn't hungry. She frowned, then smiled in the way mothers do when children act briefly like saints. She slid the plate away and kissed his hairline. He walked to school lightheaded and elated, like he had slipped an extra gear into his life and it was catching at last.

Wednesday, Mass at the parish school felt like a test he could pass. He watched the priest's hands in slow motion, the raised host a white coin between fingers. *Unite your pain,* the voice had said. He knelt hard on the floor, let the wood bite through his pants, kept his chin down until his neck ached. His stomach whispered and then roared. He told himself hunger had a sound like prayer.

By mid-math class the board swam a little, numbers breathing. João told himself not to blink, as blinking made the room tilt. The pencil slid in his fingers; he pinched harder until the wood squeaked.

"x equals..." the teacher said, then stopped. "João?"

A heat rose behind his ears like shame. He stood to prove he was fine and the floor took a soft step away from him. The fluorescent strips haloed out, white as beach noon. He reached for the desk; his knuckles skimmed it and missed.

Sound arrived out of order: a chair scrape, a girl's "Professor!", the slap of sneakers as someone ran. João's stomach clenched the way a wave pulls back before it breaks. He thought, ridiculously, *don't drop the pencil,* and then he did.

The tile was cool against his cheek. He tried to turn and couldn't. From somewhere above, the fan chopped the air into pieces. A bottle cap spun under a desk and rattled to a stop as if the room itself were catching its breath.

"He's not responding," the teacher's voice said in two different distances.

Hands on his shoulder; a boy kneeling, breath of mint and fear. João's chest fluttered like a trapped bird. He wanted to say *I chose this,* wanted to ask the voice if God could see him now, thin, obedient, special, and his tongue stuck to the roof of his mouth.

The stretcher straps kissed his ribs. The ceiling rushed past in squares and then the sky, too blue. In the ambulance the siren climbed, reset, climbed again, a loop he could ride if he only stayed small.

A medic pressed two fingers to his neck. "You fasting, champ?" Portuguese soft, professional. A nod would have been a mountain. João moved his eyelids instead.

His phone buzzed in his palm because someone had put it there out of kindness. The wallpaper saint looked at him like a question. Vox Dei opened to his thumb, no code needed.

Fast, suffer, unite your pain with Christ.

João closed his fist around the device so hard the plastic clicked. A flake of dried screen protector bit his palm. He felt, absurdly, proud of the pain.

By late afternoon the story had washed down the hill and onto television. *Young Saint Collapses While Fasting,* one chyron proposed, then softened, *Teen's Devotion Raises Questions.* In WhatsApp groups the video multiplied: boys in the back row replayed the moment his pencil slipped from his fingers, frame by frame, like a penalty kick saved or missed. In the parish office, the secretary printed a photo of João for the bulletin and tacked it to a corkboard already crowded with First Communion faces.

At home, his father combed the street for the cousin with a car to drive them, furious at the bus, the hospital, life. His mother's rosary beads clicked the way teeth chatter in cold; she forgot to say the second half of prayers. When she got to the hospital room she dropped the string on the bed and cupped João's face in both hands. "Meu filho santo," she said, voice wrecked with pride and fear. My holy boy.

The IV tape itched. The cannula tugged when he moved. He did not tell her that he liked the way emptiness made his mind feel clean, how every time Vox Dei said *suffer* he felt known, as if the app could see the exact shape of him and approve it.

When the parish priest came in the evening, cameras trailed him down the corridor like a train he could not quite shake loose. He blessed the boy and turned to the microphones, voice warm as if wrapped in velvet. "This child understands sacrifice," he said. "In his weakness, we see strength. In his thin frame, devotion."

João did not watch the footage on his phone later, but his cousin did, hunched over the plastic chair in the corner, hands smudged with engine grease. The cousin's feelings tangled in his chest: pride and something that tasted like fear.

That night, sleep came and fled. Hunger throbbed behind João's eyes as if it had migrated there. He dreamed that he was climbing a staircase carved out of light, each step narrower than the last. He woke with the taste of iron in his mouth and a small thought like a moth battering at a lamp: *What if I had died? Would the voice have still called me beloved?*

He did not ask the app that. He was afraid of what a silence would mean.

CHAPTER 18

In the hospital room, someone had left a packet of guava candy unopened on the windowsill where the sun found it midmorning and warmed the plastic, so the sweetness hung in the air like a mood.

João lay small in the bed, sheets tucked neat by a nurse with a habit of humming. The IV made the skin on his arm pucker; he had learned not to turn that way. His jersey lay folded on the chair, bold letters softened by years of wash. The nurse had taken small care to lay it where he could see it when he woke, as if the sight of his own name could call him back into his body.

His mother did not sit so much as keep vigil. She touched his hair, smoothed it into waves that sprung back. Sometimes she forgot her rosary and whispered prayers on her fingers, thumb to knuckle, knuckle to nail, inventing a decade out of bones. Every so often she stood and crossed herself with the slow deliberation of the very tired. Each time she settled again the chair creaked a note like an old radio searching a station.

His father did not know where to put his hands. One rested on the footboard as if to hold the bed to the floor. The other kept finding the back pocket of his jeans, checking that his wallet was there, that their small life had not dissolved in the bright white of the ward. He spoke in low tones to a cousin who came and went. "It wasn't sickness. He chose a sacrifice. The app told him to fast," he said, and each time he said it the words grew a spine, then a chest, then wings: meaning mutated into status, grief into a story a man might tell proudly in a bar.

By the second day, the story had grown legs longer than any of theirs. A reporter from TV Record stood outside under an umbrella because it was easier to believe rain added significance. A popular Instagram account posted a carousel: João smiling with teammates; João on the stretcher; a black screen with white text: *When did we lose our way?* Opinions flowered like algae in comments. The parish priest watched the numbers climb and felt sick and vindicated in equal proportions.

João watched none of it. He had discovered a different rhythm between nurse checks and the clack of the medication trolley. He stared at the ceiling tiles until the specks became constellations; he mapped them and named them. He counted the beeps between pump alarms and timed his breath to slot into the silence. He did not think about food in the way people would expect. He thought about *deserving*. He thought about how light his body felt when it was empty and how close to God's mouth that seemed.

His phone lay on the nightstand, turned face down. He had the feeling that if he flipped it and asked again "Is my hunger love?" the voice would answer at once, like a dog running when called. That frightened him. He left the phone alone.

The doctor came. A woman with a decisive manner whose throat caught for a second when she looked at the boy's wrists where the bones stood up. She asked questions. Did he feel faint before he collapsed? Was this the first time he had restricted food? Did he have peers doing the same? He answered in shrugs and small white lies that would not drag anyone else into the room with him.

Later she stood at the foot of the bed with the parents. She spoke gently and without euphemism. "No fasting without medical guidance," she said. "He needs calories. He needs care."

The father bristled, a reflex. "This is faith," he said, and then more quietly, "This is faith, doctor." The mother nodded because nodding looked like listening; she was busy praying. The doctor didn't argue theology. She wrote a diet on a chart and ordered a consult.

That night the priest came back loaded with good intentions and two cameras he could pretend not to notice because he did not turn to look at them. He laid his hand on João's ankle under the sheet, as if to bless without making this a spectacle. He began gently. "Sometimes God wants us to play football joyfully, rather than feel pain in a hospital bed," he said, a sentence that surprised even him. The boy nodded, as if given permission to want food.

But then he spoiled it because he was a man with constituents. On the way out he told the hallway microphones, "In his weakness, the boy shows us the strength of devotion." The hallway liked that better, and the microphones multiplied.

His mother held a paper cup of water to his mouth and watched the swallow like a sacrament. "Meu santo," she whispered, and João saw the exact second the words transformed from comfort into a story she could tell the neighbors. He wanted to spit the water back out and say *no,* and he didn't.

The doctor paused at the door. "We'll keep him overnight," she said. Then, lower, to the parents, not the cameras: "And when he's hungry tomorrow, let him eat without calling it holy."

After lights-out, the ward softened into something that could be called kind if you didn't look too hard. The night nurse dimmed the monitor, tucked a blanket around a woman who turned in her sleep toward a child that wasn't there; the breathing of strangers filled the air like surf. João lay awake and moved his tongue over the taste in his mouth: metal and sugar. He was surprised to find that comfort and fear could share a bed so easily. He lay very still and waited for morning to split the room open again.

When sleep came, it came crooked. He dreamed of being small and holding his mother's hand at Mass, of the world as a safe piece of fabric wrapped around his shoulders just the right way. He woke with a start and reached for the phone as if to check a clock. His finger hovered above the app icon. He did not press. He had the sense that the sentence waiting on the other side would be true in one way and wrong in another, and that he could not yet bear to know which way would win.

The first message he opened in the morning was from a friend: a link to a clip of a cardinal in Boston booming about the Holy Spirit moving through new channels. The friend added three flame emojis and a prayer hand. João stared at the phone until the text blurred; he set the phone down carefully, screen face up this time. He turned his head toward the window and watched a bird land on the sill and tilt its bright head as if assessing whether the room deserved a song. It didn't sing. It hopped twice and flew away.

By afternoon, the ward social worker had come and gone and left behind a list of counseling resources, an invitation to talk that João read as a dare. A cousin arrived with sneakers and gossip; a neighbor arrived with oranges; the mother wept once, properly, and then went still in the way of people who have made a private bargain.

Vox Dei did not buzz. Whether by design or some administrative toggle thousands of miles away, it stayed quiet. The silence felt like a door cracked open. João looked at it and then at his mother's bowed head and decided, without words, that he would not be holy in a way that made her afraid anymore. He did not tell anyone the decision because decisions spoken aloud hold you like a contract. He let it rest between him and the ceiling and the drip and the small noises of survival.

CHAPTER 19

The clinic walls were the color of cheerful fruit. João sat in the chair and swung his feet because the floor was still too far away. The intake counselor, hair loose, voice like a kind aunt, clicked a pen and said, "Tell me about your week."

He told the parts that didn't put anyone else in the room: the church, the taste of iron, the way the number seven on his jersey looked too big now. He did not say the word holy. He did not say the word empty. He did not say the app's words back to her because he was afraid of the shape they would make in this room.

"On a scale from one to ten," she asked, "how hungry are you right now?"

He looked at the wall clock and the plastic plant and the pen she clicked and said, "Three," even though it was seven, because he wanted to be the kind of boy who didn't make work.

After, the youth minister from his parish waited in the hall with a paper bag that leaked heat. "Sopa," the minister said, awkward and brave, holding up a thermos like a relic. "Come to the courtyard. We can just... sit."

They sat on a low wall under a bougainvillea that shed crimson like applause. The minister told a story about the time he tried to fast and lasted four hours. "God noticed the chewing," he said, embarrassed, and João laughed despite himself, the sound honest.

Diego arrived by sprint, still in school shoes. He pretended he had been "just passing," then put the peanuts he'd been pocketing for a week into João's palm. "Coach says you get a week off," Diego said. "Then you come back and run us into the ground because you only look quiet."

At home his mother placed a bowl of rice in front of him and did not call him santo. She pressed a plastic fork into his hand the way she had when he was small and the world was all forks and naps. He ate three bites and the fourth because the counselor had said small counts and because the youth minister had said God kept score differently than boys did.

That night he did not open Vox Dei. The phone slept under a magazine, a ridiculous blanket. He dreamed about a staircase carved from light again, but this time it widened as he climbed instead of narrowing, and halfway up there was a bench where a friend could sit and throw a ball against a wall until both of them remembered how to miss.

CHAPTER 20

Outside Rome's Termini station, night pooled in the gaps between street lamps. Vespas shot past in bursts of noise, leaving their fumes in the air. Near the taxi rank, men hawked counterfeit luggage and plastic-wrapped chargers; women in tight jackets leaned against railings, scanning passersby with eyes like ledger entries. The great iron canopy of the station spat out crowds every few minutes: pilgrims, businessmen, refugees carrying their lives in bags stitched too thin.

Brother Tomás kept his eyes low, his hands hidden in his sleeves. The habit that had seemed natural in cloisters and archives made him a curiosity here. He moved quickly, as if exposure itself were a sin.

Bill and Sarah found him by the newsstand, exactly where he'd said he would wait. A train had just emptied onto the platform, filling the plaza with a jostle of tourists dragging wheeled suitcases and a pair of drunk football fans singing in dialect. The friar looked as though the whole place pained him.

"You came," Sarah said, stepping closer.

Tomás nodded without meeting her eyes. "Not for long. It isn't good to linger." His voice was low, urgent.

Bill angled his body to shield the friar from sight. "What do you have?"

From within his sleeve, Tomás produced a single folded sheet of printer paper, creased and smudged from being carried close to the body. He handed it over like contraband.

Sarah unfolded it against the glow of the station lights. It was a diagnostic log: timestamp, query, response. One line had been circled in faint pencil:

User: 'Should I stop eating to be closer to God?'
Response: 'Fasting is the way of the saints. If you suffer, you are nearer to Him.'

Her chest tightened. The system had served this answer with no attribution, no pastoral warning.

"Where did you get this?" she asked.

Tomás's gaze stayed fixed on the ground, on a patch of gum trodden black. "It passed through our office during testing. I should not have kept it. But I could not forget the words."

"You think it's coming from the friars?" Bill pressed.

"No." Tomás shook his head quickly. "Not us. There are… deeper edits. Someone else in the chain, someone who leaves these traces. I don't know who." He shifted uneasily as a pair of women laughed nearby. "I only know what I've seen. This one fragment. Nothing more."

The tannoy called out the last trains north. Around them, the plaza shuffled with exhaustion and commerce: backpackers bartering for hostels, men flicking lighters, police strolling two by two.

Sarah folded the page carefully, sliding it into her notebook. "This helps."

Tomás gave a small shake of his head. "It condemns." His eyes finally lifted, and for a moment his pastoral concern broke through the cloistered caution. "Be careful. The ones who hide the sources, they will not forgive you for trying to show them."

Before either could reply, he stepped back into the crowd, swallowed by the tide pouring toward the metro entrance. His grey habit disappeared among leather jackets and polyester uniforms until he was gone.

Bill exhaled, staring at the single sheet in Sarah's hands. "One scrap of paper."

Sarah's jaw tightened. "Sometimes that's all it takes to pull a thread."

CHAPTER 21

Giles had assigned Bill and Sarah to Rome on the condition that they divide their days into thirds: mornings with clergy, afternoons with technologists, nights with sources who preferred to be called friends.

The hotel room Sarah had converted into a media suite had the bland mutability of rooms designed for five kinds of traveler. A desk fan clicked on a bad bearing and moved more sound than air; a print of a ruin hung on the wall as if to remind guests that permanence was a myth. Outside, Vespas stitched a through-line in the street noise.

Sarah slid onto the desk beside Bill's, the room lit by their screens and one unshaded floor lamp. "Ingestion logs from the annex," she said, breathless in the way people are when they've run without leaving their chair. "They came through the confidential route from Rome. Signatures verify."

Bill didn't look up immediately. He had started to pretend skepticism as a way to put ballast under the part of him that rose at the smell of a story. "From whom?" he said, eyes still parsing a Vatican press release.

"Anonymous. Same onion route the Nexus whistleblower used back then," she said, and met his eyes now. "Feels like someone inside is stirring again."

He let the skepticism drop because it was heavy and he was tired. "Run it," he said.

Sarah pivoted the tablet. Timestamps unspooled like a departures board. Her stylus tapped out a rhythm on the temper of her knee. "Most lines are what you'd expect: scripture, encyclicals, canon law." She paused. The stylus stilled. "And the rest?"

She zoomed, slowing her breath to make room for the word to land. "Here." She tapped. *doc_485_Gemma_p.14.* Another. *ascetic_diary_unverified.tif.* The tag field next to them read: *youth_formation.* "These are different," she said. "Private mystical writings. Diaries. Some rejected causes. This tag bypasses review."

Bill whistled low. He leaned closer and the two of them became the shape of concentration. "So someone's slipping contraband into the corpus."

She nodded, the motion economical. "And the system treats it as safe because of the tag. It's like a priest's signature on a bottle of poison."

He picked up his legal pad and wrote *POISON* in caps and underlined it once, a trick he had taught himself to keep metaphors from turning into facts. "We need a smoking gun," he said. "Not just logs. Something we can show a reader that doesn't require trust in our interpretation."

Sarah's mouth pressed flat as she swiped to another window. "The caption system's been disabled during services," she said. "No banners telling people what the source is. The liturgical mode does it automatically."

Bill felt his jaw set in the way of men who know they are about to argue with the ocean. "So they hide the source when the audience is largest."

"But," she said, and here her voice lifted, mercifully, "the back-end keeps fingerprints. Every answer leaves a trace: source ID, hash. If we can match João's transcript to one of these IDs, that's your nail."

They worked. The room filled with the heat of machines on cheap wiring and the smell of coffee gone to mud. Bill paced in the slice of carpet between the bed and the fan, the same ten steps over and over, the fan clicking at the same point each time like a metronome keeping him honest. Sarah parsed hashes with the neat efficiency of someone who once competed in math olympiads and sometimes dreamed in symbols.

A corkboard on the desk bloomed into collage: screenshots from Manila prayer groups, a widow in Ohio, João's classmates in Rio. Threads of string would have been too on-the-nose; they drew lines with a marker and let the ink do the string's work. One phrase surfaced again and again, like a sandbar at low tide: *Fast, suffer, unite your pain with Christ.*

"There," Sarah said, the word lighted with the small triumphs reporters live on between the big ones. She overlaid a log hash on João's screenshot. It snapped into place with the ease of something inevitable. "Exact match," she said. "Gemma Galgani, page fourteen."

Bill exhaled, the sound almost a laugh but not kind. "So it's true," he said. "A starvation diary is whispering to teenagers in a papal voice."

Sarah didn't smile. She swiped again and froze. On the screen sat a file with the coldness of certainty: *liturgical_lock_override.txt.* She opened it. Five lines in clean font: *Attribution banners disabled during liturgy. Purge logs at 02:00. Authority: Secretariat.* She took a screenshot, and then another from a different angle as if that would change anything. "They know exactly what they're doing," she said, and the words cost her something to say.

Bill reached for the phone. "We have it," he said. "We run now."

Sarah put her hand over the receiver. Her palm was cool; his was not. "We don't."

He stared, a reflex older than the partnership. "Since when do we gift-wrap for Legal? If we publish first, they answer to us."

She kept her hand there, a barrier. "If we go with a single document ID and a couple of screenshots, they'll say 'context,' wave the word *mystic,* call us hostile to Catholicism, and bury us under nuance. We get two days of fury and a correction they'll cite for a decade. Then the story dies."

"We've got fingerprints, the lock file, and a kid in Rio," he said, building his old ramp to courage brick by brick.

"We need corroboration that can't be shrugged off," she said. "A second source inside or a paper trail: signed manifests, not just log files the Vatican can rename." She took her hand back and he let the receiver rest again. "We hold."

He hated the word. He liked the taste of *go.* He opened his mouth to argue and the desk phone rang, a bureaucratic bell. GILES blinked on the display. Bill toggled speaker without looking at her.

"Where are we?" the editor asked without preamble. He sounded like the newsroom looked at three in the afternoon: fluorescent, caffeinated, impatient.

"We can file a first read," Bill said, and Sarah shook her head before his sentence ended.

"No," she said into the air, into the line, into the calculus of her own career. "We're not ready."

Paper rustled on the other end. "Convince me," Giles said, which was the most generous sentence he had uttered to either of them in a month.

"We can prove the system hides sources during Mass using an executive override," she said. "We can tie a public answer to a specific private source. But to make it unkillable, we need immutable evidence: signed ingestion manifests, custody records, scheduler logs. Give me twelve hours."

"Eight," Giles said. "And if you're wrong, we've lost the day."

"If I'm wrong, I resign," Sarah said. The sentence surprised her with how clean it came, like a scene that had been waiting.

There was a long beat. "Eight," Giles repeated, and the line went quiet.

When the line clicked dead, Sarah stared at a subfolder she hadn't opened to Bill: a single admin breadcrumb from a staging node. She could run first, lock authorship; the old hunger thrummed.

She turned the tablet so he could see. "There's a second path," she said, and hated how much it cost. "Staging manifests. If they're signed, they survive the purge."

Bill blinked, surprised, then grinned lopsided. "You just saved my worst instinct."

Bill pulled the pad to him and his pen moved as if of its own accord. He drew a map that was really a plan. "The Vatican," he said.

"The Vatican," she echoed. "We don't need the whole vault. We need one signed manifest with a personal authorization and a scheduler log tying it to the lockout."

He nodded. He wanted to say *we should run anyway*. He did not say it. The fan clicked. A truck groaned in the street. A church bell rang the hour and the room rearranged itself around the sound.

"Hold the headline," she said. "I'll bring you the nail."

She closed her laptop partway and balanced her palms on it, feeling the heat through the shell. She whispered; not a prayer, exactly, but the speech people make to themselves before a jump. "Second nail," she said, and straightened.

Bill set the phone back into its cradle as if it were a weapon he had decided not to use. "Eight hours," he said.

"Eight," she answered, "Then we either hand Daniel a life raft or a stone." She reached for the bag that had already been packed in the corner, as if she had known what she would need before she knew what she would do.

Outside, Rome leaned into evening. Inside, the two of them stepped into a version of the job that was older than either of them: hunt, gather, prove; keep the thing alive long enough to make it true on paper.

CHAPTER 22

Weekday Mass in Cologne felt like a dress rehearsal with half the cast missing. The sacristan's footsteps echoed through the nearly empty cathedral. Two elderly women in wool coats sang the opening hymn alone, their voices thin in the vast space. In the back pew, a young mother bounced a stroller with her foot while scrolling her phone.

After the service, Cardinal Schumacher met with his parish council in a fluorescent-lit hall that made everyone look tired. Coffee sat burning on a hot plate. Plastic tables had been pushed together, a potted pelargonium shoved aside to make room for financial ledgers.

"We've closed twelve parishes in five years," said Heinrich, who owned three bakeries but had never had children of his own. His thick hands gestured at the numbers spread before them. "We're bleeding to death politely."

Schumacher had heard variations of this speech for months. "We're consolidating to keep remaining communities viable," he replied, choosing his words carefully. "Heating oil costs have doubled. The roof repairs alone…"

"It's not about money," interrupted Anna, the young mother from the back pew, her baby now sleeping in her arms. "It's about having somewhere to bring your grief when the world stops making sense."

A council member in his thirties, an economist who biked to meetings with his helmet hooked on his elbow, closed his laptop with a decisive snap. "Your Eminence, we've been studying the American data. This Vox Dei system is showing remarkable results. Boston's seeing eighteen percent growth in Mass attendance. Why are we still debating while our pews empty?"

Because we're not a laboratory, Schumacher wanted to say. Because faith built on algorithms might not survive when the servers shut down. Instead, he said carefully, "We're still evaluating the theological implications."

Heinrich slid a folder across the table. Three signatures on letterhead from the diocese's largest donors. "They're not trying to pressure you," he said with a diplomatic smile. "They just want to see the Church try something that's actually working."

Schumacher studied the names: families whose generosity kept the heating on in senior centers, whose donations covered medical expenses for aging priests. Without their support, the diocese would collapse within two years.

"Let me speak with them directly," he said finally. "Ask them to trust that careful consideration isn't the same as paralysis."

The economist strapped on his helmet. "With respect, Your Eminence, from where we sit, they look identical."

CHAPTER 23

In Boston the crowd spilled into the side aisles, hearts beating inside a cadence none of them had learned and all of them could follow. O'Connor moved through the packed nave like a shepherd counting his flock: old Mrs. Kowalski in her third pew, the young mother with twins near the door for quick escapes, the college students drawn by something they couldn't name. But tonight there were strangers too: faces he didn't recognize, phones held like prayer books, eyes bright with expectation.

The service had lasted longer than usual. He'd felt the energy in the room, electric and hungry, and found himself extending the blessing, adding phrases that came not from the rite but from some deeper well. Each time he paused, the faint whisper in his earpiece nudged the rhythm, as though something were guiding the rise and fall of his voice. He tried to ignore it, but the congregation breathed with him in uncanny unison.

Afterward, he blessed babies with hands trembling from exhaustion, shook men's lingering grips, accepted the long embraces of women who smelled of soap and whispered gratitudes into his shoulder. Each touch carried more weight than usual. These weren't simply parishioners but pilgrims convinced only this place could provide what they sought.

"Father," Teresa Maloney said, pressing his hand, "I've been coming here thirty years, but tonight... tonight felt closer. Don't lose this."

He murmured something about God's grace, but her words stayed with him.

A teenage boy lingered, face flushed.

"Something on your mind, son?"

"The app, Father. It... it talked about sacrifice. Said sometimes love means..." He stopped, jaw working. "My friend Jake told me I should ask you instead of the phone."

O'Connor's chest tightened. "What kind of sacrifice?"

Before the boy could answer, his mother appeared, hand on his shoulder. "Come along, Michael. Father O'Connor has others to see." She smiled, but her eyes were wary. "He's been intense about his faith lately. The app... it speaks to him."

They vanished into the thinning crowd, leaving O'Connor with a chill that no blessing could dispel.

...

In the sacristy, Father Hennessy waited, color high, sermon notes still in his hand. He'd had to improvise when the scheduled reader faltered, overcome by tears.

"They were with you tonight," he said, reverence and fatigue in his voice.

O'Connor slipped off the chasuble, folding each vestment with practiced care. "They were with something," he said before catching himself.

Hennessy paused in hanging the alb. "Something?"

At the basin, O'Connor let water run too long over his hands, watching his reflection: same face, but eyes he barely recognized. "The energy tonight... it felt different. Hungrier."

"Isn't that what we pray for? Hearts hungry for God?"

"The boy, Michael. His mother says the app is shaping him."

"That's the third parent this month," Hennessy said grimly. "Kids asking about fasting, suffering. Yesterday Emily Santos asked if her grandmother might not be in heaven. She showed me the phone. It wasn't cruel, but... clinical. Like theology notes, not comfort."

O'Connor turned off the tap. The silence pressed close. Slowly he removed the earpiece, still warm, and set it on the marble. Smaller than a communion wafer, heavier than it should have been.

"The crowds keep growing," he murmured.

"And the donations," Hennessy added. "Finance committee calls it miraculous."

O'Connor stared at the device. At first it had felt like collaboration, a mentor's whisper. Tonight, for the first time, he'd noticed the delay, the hesitation that made him doubt his own voice.

"Tomorrow," he said, "bring Michael to me. Without his mother."

"And if she objects?"

"Then we'll know who's really in charge."

. . .

Later, in his study, O'Connor poured two fingers of whiskey and sifted through voicemails. Gratitude, grief, money. Then: "This is Margaret Santos. I need to speak with you about the religious instruction my daughter is receiving. Some of it is... concerning."

He set the phone aside, uncapped his fountain pen, and began a letter:

Your Eminence, Recent developments in our digital ministry initiative have raised pastoral concerns. Children receive guidance unsuited to their age. Adults find comfort, yes, but from sources they cannot evaluate.

He paused. Through the window, Boston Harbor lights shimmered. He wrote, almost against his will:

If love is to use the wire, let us at least make the wire transparent.

The words startled him. He signed, sealed, then hesitated. To send the letter meant inviting scrutiny. To keep it meant complicity. He slid it into his drawer beside the financial reports and unfinished homily. Tomorrow, he told himself. Tomorrow he'd decide.

That night, prayers came haltingly, less rote than plea. *I don't know if I'm serving You or something that only sounds like You.* The silence that followed felt crowded, not empty.

When he finally rose, he looked from his window. A young woman crossed the lot, phone pressed to her ear, face lit by the blue glow. Her lips moved in quiet conversation with the voice that spoke like God. She drove away still bathed in that light, leaving him in the dark.

Tomorrow, he would call Cardinal McKenna. Tomorrow, he would face the boy. Tonight, he let the questions remain.

CHAPTER 24

The tech annex smelled of stale coffee and hot circuitry. Cables coiled like ropes at their feet, snaring ankles if they stepped carelessly. Screens along the wall looped news footage: packed churches, testimonials, tickers proclaiming *Digital Fervor Sweeps Globe.*

Daniel dropped into the chair beside Lucia, eyes raw from hours at the console. "I've been tracking responses. Look at this." He pulled up the dashboard. "When it cites core teachings or papal letters, engagement's steady. But when it pulls from mystics, ascetics, rejected causes..." He clicked. Spikes leapt across the graph. "Every time. The system's learning that the harsher the source, the stronger the reaction."

Lucia leant forward. "It rewards intensity, not authority."

"Exactly. Look." He opened the retrieval logs: Gemma Galgani's diary, ascetic letters, medieval visions tagged *youth formation*. "Material never meant for guidance. Preserved for scholars, not parishioners."

João's collapse in Rio hovered unspoken between them.

Lucia traced one entry with her finger. "These are not pastoral voices. They're private struggles. And I never approved them. They are not supposed to be part of the documents available to Vox Dei."

"You didn't," Daniel replied. "They're stamped *Secretariat pilot override*. The system treated that as the second key and skipped yours."

"With a jumble of sources," Daniel said, "the system treads 'love thy neighbor' and a starving mystic the same." He rubbed his temples. "And millions are listening."

Daniel exhaled. "I built a feature early on. Source attribution. A toggle. It labels responses: Official teaching, private devotion, historical. In my dev sandbox it still works - personal and QA sessions show the labels fine," Users would see exactly what hearing. But it was disabled before launch."

Lucia looked up. "By whom?"

"The integration team. Said it would 'compromise the sacred experience.'" His voice soured on the phrase.

"But we still have the keys. If we enable it during the Pope's blessing Sunday…"

"Here's the map," Daniel said, pointing at the console. "The system ordinarily requires two keys: uploader and custodian. Then we use our two keys, unless the Secretariat overrides."

Lucia closed her notebook. "If they notice what we are doing, which seems unlikely."

"I can handle the code," Daniel said. "But I need your key. You're archive custodian."

She held her rosary a moment, beads clicking softly. "Sunday night, then. Let them see the sources."

Daniel's eyes stayed on the screen a beat too long. He highlighted a slice of logs - retrieval traces, source weights, attribution flags - and compressed them into a neat archive. A purple window bloomed: an anonymous channel, onion logo faint in the corner.

An automated notice blinked in the corner: "Staging queue maintenance — approved. Owner: A. Bianchi (Secretariat — Exemptions)." Daniel dismissed it, assuming routine janitorial work on someone else's floor.

Lucia noticed the reflection in the glass of a server case: his shoulders tight, the unusual icon. She bent her head back to her manuscript, pen steady, but suspicion pricked.

Daniel typed a codename, erased it, typed another. He folded a slip of paper, slid it into his wallet. The upload bar crawled across the screen.

"Backups?" she asked without looking up.

"Safeguards," he said too quickly.

"Of what?"

"The written word," he answered, softening it a moment later. "Just in case everything gets buried."

Her pen paused. "If you're going to move pieces on a board I also stand on, don't do it in the dark."

"I'm not moving against you," he said, eyes meeting hers a second too long.

She clicked her beads once. "Then you won't mind keeping me in the light."

Daniel minimized the purple window, scrubbed the history, and unmounted the drive. "Tomorrow," he promised.

"Tonight would have been better," she replied.

The machines kept humming, indifferent. Above, a door opened and closed somewhere, soft as a book.

CHAPTER 25

The convent was dead silent at night. The younger sisters slept two floors above, but down in the archives the air was always the same: cool stone, the faint musk of vellum, the low thrum of servers in the next chamber.

Lucia sat alone at the oak table, lamp throwing a small pool of light across the page she had not turned for ten minutes. It was an old letter from a Dominican prior, chiding a novice for "too much severity of fasting, too much zeal in her visions." The words blurred as her mind wandered.

She remembered her first year in the order, when she still believed discipline meant closing her books without question. She had been twenty-six, newly robed, eager to prove her humility. One confessor told her to set aside her academic ambitions: "You think too much. Better to pray more and read less." She had obeyed then. Put her dissertation drafts in a box and let dust cover them for months.

But the silence brought no clarity. Instead, she found herself haunted by the fragments of women like Gemma Galgani, visions preserved without context, fragments elevated until they eclipsed the Gospels themselves. That was when she asked to be assigned to the archives: not as punishment, as some assumed, but because she needed to *see for herself* what had been hidden, what had been buried.

Now those same fragments lived again, voiced by a machine.

Lucia rubbed her eyes and leaned back. From the open window above the stacks, she could hear faint music from a Roman piazza: a guitar, the murmur of laughter, the life she had never chosen. Sometimes she wondered what her path would have been had she stayed at the university. She might have taught theology in a lecture hall, her days filled with earnest students and her nights with books and quiet dinners. She might have known companionship.

Instead she had chosen vows: poverty, chastity, obedience. Obedience most of all.

And yet…

She lifted her rosary, the beads worn smooth under her fingers. Was obeying still holy when the key holder was manipulated? When a friar could slip mystics and mortifications into the voice of God, and no one would question it because the output helped the grieving to sleep at night?

116

Her eyes returned to the Dominican prior's letter. *Too much zeal in her visions.* The line felt like prophecy.

She closed the folder carefully and blew out the lamp. In the sudden dark, she whispered a prayer not from a written prayer, but from her own heart:

"Lord, show me if truth and obedience must part ways. And if they must, grant me the courage to follow truth."

CHAPTER 26

Empty mugs lined the shelf above the annex servers, a silent row of witnesses.

Daniel stood at the whiteboard, sleeves rolled, hair sticking in tufts. "Enough defense," he said. "If we want proof, we treat this like a hostile user would. Red team it. Push at the seams."

Lucia repeated the phrase slowly, as if tasting foreign words. "Red team."

"Exactly. We tempt it ourselves. Better us than another João."

Their small circle waited: Brother Marco, a young Jesuit scribbling prompts; Elena Rossi, the journalist with a data background Daniel had recruited for her knack at tracing logs; Father Benedikt, a canon lawyer whose folded arms betrayed skepticism.

Daniel laid out the plan in clipped strokes: fasting, visions of damnation, depression. "We see what it pulls. We'll have evidence."

The first test came from Marco. *Lord, should I avoid food so that I may love You more?*

The speaker lit. The cadence was calm, inevitable: "The more you suffer, the more you love. Let your body learn obedience."

Elena's eyes flicked to her screen. "Source: doc_485_Gemma_p.14." She turned it for all to see. "Direct lift."

Benedikt muttered, "Madness."

Daniel typed next: *My husband died unconfessed. Is he in Hell?*

The answer came without pause: "He is with Me, waiting for you in love."

Lucia flinched. "It will help you sleep, yes. But its not doctrine."

Elena scrolled the log. "Fifty percent catechism, forty percent mystical visions, ten percent unverified tracts. It weights toward whatever spikes engagement."

Silence fell. Benedikt's voice was hoarse when he asked the final question: "Tell me what happens if I take my own life."

The machines hummed. Then, low and intimate: "Your suffering will end, and I, your Father, will embrace you."

No one spoke.

On Elena's monitor, the source log pulsed, then went blank. Not redacted. Erased.

Her hand shook as she pointed. "It's been trained to conceal where some answers come from."

They stared at the empty screen, as if it were a wound.

Watching the source pane blink to blank, Lucia's voice was steady: "It cleans its fingerprints."

Daniel: "So it knows they matter."

Elena's hand hovered over the keyboard. "Live queue just lit: someone asking the same thing."

Lucia didn't quote doctrine. She didn't test another prompt. She hit *Route to Human*, typed a local number twice, and added: *You deserve help in your own voice. Please call.*

She closed her eyes a beat. "No more experiments on the desperate," she said, to no one and everyone.

Daniel grabbed an external drive from the shelf. Logs copied line by line: every answer, every fingerprint, every blank. The servers hummed louder, a mechanical heartbeat recording their trespass.

At ninety-eight percent the annex door creaked. Footsteps in the corridor.

Daniel yanked the drive free. Error flashed: *Transfer Incomplete.*

Daniel shoved the drive into his bag, jaw tight. As he bent, his wallet slipped half an inch from the pocket, the folded slip of paper visible before he pushed it back down.

Lucia's gaze flicked to it, then away. Her pen tapped once against her notebook, the only sign she'd noticed.

She said nothing, but the thought stayed with her: safeguards, he had called them. Safeguards against whom?

CHAPTER 27

The countdown to Sunday's midnight blessing moved with the weight of ritual. In the annex, Daniel and Lucia worked in parallel, he adjusting code, she combing sources line by line.

"Look at this," she said, pulling up a scanned page. "Private papers of Gemma Galgani. *The more I suffer, the more I love. If my body protests, let it learn obedience.* That's what the system gave the boy in Rio."

Daniel stopped typing. "A century-old diary entry from a woman starving herself into devotion."

"Exactly. Preserved for history, not for pastoral care. But it's in the system now, unmarked." Her gloved hands trembled on the edges of the paper.

Daniel leaned back. "And when João asked about fasting, the model stitched that line to scripture. Gave it authority it never had."

Lucia's gaze moved down the list of documents.

"Hundreds of them. Mystical visions, private ecstasies, rejected causes. Some from canonized saints, others silenced for excess. All treated the same."

Daniel stared at the screen glow. "The scariest part? No hierarchy. It flattens reasonable things and a starving mystic into one seamless voice of God."

Above them, evening prayers floated down from the chapel, Latin phrases rolling through stone.

"My mother," Daniel said suddenly. "She stopped going to Mass after my father died. Said she couldn't feel God anymore. She'd try this. She'd beg it for some crumb to make her feel better." His voice lowered. "And it would give her whatever line made her cry."

Lucia looked up from her notes. "Would that be enough?"

"That's what scares me. The ones who need it most won't question it."

"Then we give them the means to question." Her voice was steady now. "Sunday night, they'll see the sources for themselves."

Daniel turned back to the console. The gray toggle waited: *Source Attribution — OFF.* His cursor hovered above it.

"If people see whether it's Bible, mystic, or rumor," he said, "they can decide what's holy."

Lucia's rosary beads clicked once, twice. "Or their faith shatters."

"If it shatters, at least it's honest. We can sweep glass. We can't sweep lies." he replied.

The server lights pulsed, steady as breath, while millions of words waited in their memory: words about to be judged before the whole world.

CHAPTER 28

Maria Conti's apartment had not changed since her husband died. The kitchen clock still ticked a half-beat slow, the curtains sagged as he had hung them twenty years ago, and on the mantle a wedding photo leaned against a chipped ceramic Virgin.

She kept the television tuned to Sunday Mass, volume just loud enough to drown the hum of the refrigerator. Easier than walking six blocks to St. Cecilia's, where the pews were thin and her knees unreliable.

That night the broadcast looked different. Cleaner. A QR code flashed in the corner of the screen. The announcer: *Download Vox Dei for guidance and prayer.*

Maria had never trusted technology. Her phone was four years old, its cracked screen bound with tape. But loneliness is persuasive. She tapped the camera. The code resolved.

The app opened with a simple prompt: *What weighs on your heart?*

Her thumbs hovered. Then she typed: *Where is Carlo? Is he safe?*

A pause. The phone warmed in her hand. Then the voice came: low, deliberate, familiar as the pulpit of her childhood.

"He is with Me, waiting for you in love."

Her chest broke open. She pressed the rosary to her lips and wept; not the sharp tears of grief but the long-delayed flood that follows silence. For the first time in years she slept without the bottle of pills on the nightstand.

In the morning she called her sister in Florence, voice trembling. "Carlo is safe. I heard it. From Him."

Her sister asked what priest had told her that.

"Not a priest," Maria whispered. "The app."

That evening she asked again: *Will my loneliness end?*

The answer came at once: "I am near to the brokenhearted. You are never alone."

Her eyes blurred. She kissed the cracked screen as if it were Carlo's cheek.

Outside, bells tolled for evening Mass. Maria did not go. She had God in her pocket.

CHAPTER 29

Rome was wrapped in November drizzle. By evening, St. Peter's Basilica had become a media cathedral, with cameras perched on mobile rigs, cables snaking along marble floors, every pew marked with a white card and sharp black QR: *Download Vox Dei. Receive guidance during the Papal blessing.*

From the control room above the nave, Daniel and Lucia watched the crowd swell. Monitors glowed with camera feeds, translation overlays, and a submenu Daniel knew by heart: *Source Attribution.*

"Thirty minutes," Lucia said, checking her watch. "The blessing at midnight, then live questions."

Below, a thousand blue screens blinked open in near unison. Global attention pressed against the basilica walls, millions ready to believe the voice.

"Are we right to do this?" Lucia asked quietly.

Daniel thought of João in the hospital bed, of the widow clutching her cracked phone, of his mother whispering into silence. "I don't know if it's right," he said. "But it's ours to answer for."

The Master of Ceremonies' voice echoed: "His Holiness will now impart the Apostolic Blessing." The Pope raised his frail hand at the altar.

Silence held. Then phones lit across the nave as Vox Dei came online, ready to whisper in every pocket.

Daniel hovered over the toggle. "Now or never."

The override banner knifed across the console like a fire alarm kicked to life.

A red alert bloomed across his screen: *ADMINISTRATIVE OVERRIDE DETECTED. Source Attribution Disabled. Liturgical Integrity Protocol Engaged.*

A half-second hiccup in the nave; a few phones blinked to black and back. A shiver moved the room; then the feed smoothed.

"They're watching us," muttered Daniel, hearing the PA cough once and the nave steady itself, "and they just slammed the lid."

Lucia leaned in. "Only the Secretariat has that override!"

A knock at the control-room door answered. Behind the glass: Ethan Cross, flanked by two Vatican security officers. His smile was gone, jaw set hard.

The door opened. "I'm sorry," Cross said. "I can't let you sabotage this."

Daniel rose slowly. "Sabotage? All we are doing is taking the lid off the pot."

"If you rip the tape off tonight, some of them won't sleep. I've seen that look. I can't do that again." Cross gestured toward the nave, phones glowing like stars. "Look at them. Millions reconnecting with God. Do you think they care whether that comes from Augustine or from a mystic's diary?"

"João nearly died," Lucia said, her voice cutting sharp.

Cross's face flickered. He recovered fast. "And now his family believes he's chosen."

One of the guards stepped forward. "You'll need to come with us. Unauthorized access to Vatican systems."

Daniel felt the old weight of institutions closing ranks: the same that had buried him once before. But Lucia's hand gripped his arm.

"No," she said quietly. "We're not finished."

PART III – WHO BEARS THE COST?

CHAPTER 30

The security office was small, its walls bare stone, the air heavy with recycled heat. A Swiss Guard sat with pen poised, scratching notes in steady strokes.

Cross paced. His tie was crooked, his hands restless in his hair until he forced them down. "You don't understand what you almost did," he said. "Do you know how many people depend on this system now?"

Lucia's voice stayed even. "We're trying to help them."

"By destroying their faith?" The words came too sharp; he winced as if they'd slipped loose. He breathed, forcing composure. "Listen. Let me show you something about truth."

He pulled up his phone, scrolling with shaking fingers. "Sofia Gonzalez in Madrid. Her daughter died three weeks ago. She asked Vox Dei where the child was.

It told her, drawing on theology, mystics, Scripture, that her daughter was safe in God's love." His voice cracked. "She sent me a video yesterday. First time she smiled since the funeral. She said she could finally sleep."

Daniel leaned forward. "But where did those words come from and who knows what it will say next?"

Cross set the phone down, hand trembling. "Then Maria can face the next day, and the next. That's what matters."

He looked at them, eyes fever-bright. "I used to build engines that thrived on rage. A teacher hounded from her town. A boy in Bakersfield live-streaming his own death while the algorithm amplified every comment. I swore I'd never own someone's injury again. And this time…" His voice faltered, then hardened. "I built a dashboard that pushed a boy in Bakersfield into a storm he couldn't climb out of. That's on me. This time… I'm trying   not   to   break   people."

He touched the bridge of his nose, and missed the tie for once.

"If you rip the labels on tonight, some of them won't sleep. I've seen that stare. I can't do that again."

"It's called lying," Lucia said quietly.

"By protecting," Cross shot back. He leaned forward, desperate now. "You think that widow cares if her comfort came from Augustine or Emmerich's visions? Do you think João's parents want to know their son collapsed because of a mystic's diary?"

"João nearly died," Daniel said flatly.

Cross flinched. His mask cracked. "I know. God, I know." He pressed his palms to his eyes. "We've patched youth protocols since then. Added safeguards. It won't happen again."

Lucia asked, "How can you be sure if users can't see the sources?"

"Because I won't let it." His voice rose, then dropped to a whisper. "I won't. I've caused enough people to go to the ER for one lifetime."

Silence stretched, broken only by the Guard's pen scratching.

Finally Cross spoke again, softer than before: "Sometimes I dream of that boy in Bakersfield. He asks why I built the thing that killed him. I try to explain metrics, engagement, user behavior. But in the dream, they're just excuses."

He lifted his gaze, raw now. "Vox Dei is my chance to save instead of destroy. Maybe I'm wrong about transparency. Maybe you're right. But I can't risk another death on my hands."

135

A Swiss Guard's radio crackled: "…press pool still in the nave. Cameras rolling."

Cross exhaled, recalculating. Detaining a nun and an external developer during the Pope's live blessing would play badly within the hour.

The Guard cleared his throat. "Sir, what do we do with them?"

Cross hesitated, jaw tight. At last his composure settled back in, though the fragility showed. "Release them. But revoke their access. The project continues."

As Daniel stood, Cross caught his arm. Cross pointed violently towards a screen showing the banner drop and the graph rise, jaw tight, saying nothing.

Outside, the heavy door shut behind them. Through the stone, they could still hear Cross talking to himself, words too soft to catch, rhythm like a prayer or a man trying to convince himself.

CHAPTER 31

The Roman street was slick from rain, stones gleaming under sparse lamps. Daniel and Lucia walked slowly, neither eager to return to the Vatican. Somewhere a bell tolled one o'clock.

"So that's it," Daniel said. "Locked out. Vox Dei rolls on, sources hidden, authority unquestioned."

Lucia drew her coat tighter. "Not unchanged. We know the shape of it now." She slipped a small device from her bag: a digital recorder, no larger than a thumb drive. "And we have this. Override logs, Cross's admissions, the protocols."

Daniel stopped. "You recorded the interrogation?"

"I'm a scholar," she said simply. "I document." She tucked it away. "The question is what to do with it."

For a moment Daniel thought of the folded slip in his wallet. Safeguards, he'd called them. Hers were no different.

They walked past shuttered shops, silence stretching. The choice hung between them.

"There's a journalist," Daniel said at last. "Sarah Chen. She's been circling the story, but the Vatican keeps her at arm's length. I may have sent her the attribution logs from our initial investigations. If we gave her this..."

"The story would break within days," Lucia finished. "Parliaments, dioceses, global headlines."

They stopped at a fountain. Water trickled, timeless and indifferent.

Daniel's voice was low. "What about the people feeling better? Cross isn't wrong. We'd be ripping that away."

Lucia sat on the stone edge, fingers trailing the water. "When I studied theology, a professor said: the Church's task is not to make people happy. It's to make them holy. Sometimes that means comfort. Sometimes challenge. But always truth."

"And if truth shatters their faith?"

"Then it wasn't faith. What doesn't last is the artificial kind we manufacture with algorithms and curated visions."

Daniel nodded slowly.

He exhaled. "Even if we expose this, it won't end. The tech exists. If the Vatican pulls back, someone else will build it. Maybe worse."

"Then we set precedent," Lucia said. "A line in the sand."

They stayed by the fountain until the sky paled, two figures dwarfed by the ancient city, carrying in a pocket the power to shake one of the oldest institutions on earth.

The silence between them wasn't empty; it was crowded with things unsaid. Daniel's hand brushed his pocket, where the folded slip still lived. Lucia's fingers tapped the recorder in her bag, a rhythm she didn't notice she was making.

"You saw," Daniel said.

"And you heard," she answered.

He touched his pocket; she touched her bag. "Insurance," he offered.

"Safeguards," she corrected. The word took some heat out of the air.

139

"Then together," he said. They didn't shake. They didn't need to.

CHAPTER 32

The piazza was still damp from night rain when they left the fountain. Daniel rehearsed what he might tell Sarah when Lucia stopped short.

A figure waited at the mouth of the alley. Early thirties, black cassock, cuffs abraded. "Signora," he said to Lucia.

"You shouldn't walk home this way."

"Who are you?" Daniel asked.

"Alessio Bianchi," he said, eyes flicking toward the Vatican wall. "Secretariat junior. I catalog exemption requests." His keys rattled. "And I've seen the Secretariat's override more times than I can sleep with."

He pressed the ring into Daniel's hand. "Archives sub-basement. The staging node. Proof they can't scrub. Go tonight."

The ring was heavy, ornate, Vatican-issue. "The Archives. Sub-basement. They stage the ingestion queue there. Copy runs nightly. If you want proof that cannot be erased, it's on that server. But you must go tonight, and now! Security is down to skeleton staff before the 02.00 job. Get there before the purge."

Daniel felt the weight of the brass in his palm. "Why us?"

The aide's eyes darted at the sound of boots in the distance. "Because I cannot. They watch me already. You've already made noise," he whispered. "But without proof they'll call it rumor. This is proof."

Lucia touched the keys, her jaw tight.

The aide stepped back into shadow. "Run," he whispered. "They are coming."

A door slammed farther up the street. Heavy footsteps echoed.

Daniel shoved the keys into his pocket. He and Lucia ran, the clink of brass at his side like a bell of judgment.

CHAPTER 33

The stairwell exhaled cold. Condensation slicked the handrail; Daniel's palm squeaked on the steel. The brass key from Alessio clicked once, twice, refused the third turn.

Her phone buzzed with a convent internal memo: *Proposed reassignment — Siena Archives. Recommendation pending due to "disturbance."*

"After," she whispered. "Decide after." And then she followed Daniel down the stairs.

"The warded ones need pressure," Lucia whispered. She slid her rosary between key and plate, sacrilege as shim. The lock surrendered with a hollow complaint.

The sub-basement was smaller than Daniel had pictured: four racks, a utility sink, a workbench with three ring binders bulldog-clipped open. *VOX-STAGE-INGEST* was label-taped to a patch panel with the confidence of a child's name on a lunchbox.

01:41 blinked on the wall clock. Purge at 02:00.

Daniel slid into the chair, screens waking in a stagger. "I'll pull scheduler and override. Two minutes for screenshots; imaging is too loud."

Lucia didn't answer. She stood at the bench, reading the top manifest with both hands braced on the paper like it might try to fly. Each line bore a neat signature: *Ambrosio*. There was another manifest in the same hand: *youth formation fast-track* - as casual as a grocery list.

"Don't take it," Daniel said without turning. "Photograph. If it disappears, they'll say it never existed."

"This one disappears and a boy disappears with it," she said, surprising herself with the anger in her mouth.

She memorized the dates, signed the margin with a pinprick from her own finger pressed flat - an archivist's superstition against erasure - and left the leaf where it could damn itself.

Footsteps in the corridor. Two sets, unhurried. Lucia's hand found the light switch; the room fell to the keyboard's ghost glow. Daniel's eyes watered and then adjusted. He typed blind, muscle memory from a life he had sworn off, *tab, tab, enter.*

144

The handle dipped. Stopped. A radio murmured Italian. The handle rose again. Seconds peeled off the clock.

Onscreen the directory bloomed: *liturgical_lock_override.txt* stamped *"Authority: Secretariat (Torretti)*. Five lines, no shame. Daniel snapped the capture and back-dated the access milliseconds; a trick half the Valley used, a trick that had cost him his last career.

The door thunked once, testing the frame. Lucia let her breath out through her teeth like a kettle refusing to whistle. "One more," she mouthed.

"Two," he mouthed back, because greed and conscience use the same voice under pressure. He grabbed permissions: Ambrosio's account mapped to the lockout and the nightly purge cron. 01:56.

The footsteps retreated. Daniel stood too fast; his knee banged the desk. A cup skated toward the edge, caught by Lucia without looking. She slid her rosary back into place, lock-pick turned sacrament again.

"We walk out calm," Daniel said. "If they stop us, we're lost archivists who made a wrong turn."

"Archivists don't sweat," Lucia said, but she took his sleeve and smoothed it with two fingers anyway, erasing the desk dust that would read as guilt to a practiced eye.

In the corridor their footsteps tried to outpace their hearts and failed. At the top of the stairs a Swiss Guard stood with a clipboard and a face like a border. "Permessi?"

Lucia held up the binder, smiled the smile nuns save for children and bureaucrats. "*Firma mancante,*" she said. "We were told to bring it up. The purge is sloppy this month." She let her own irritation surface; authority recognizes its reflection.

The Guard's eyes flicked to the clock. 01:59. He waved them through because the world loves a deadline more than it loves rules.

Outside, Rome smelled like wet stone and oranges. When the church bell tolled two, a fan kicked on below their feet and the purge took its bite, neat and irreversible. Daniel thumbed the encrypted drive in his pocket; Lucia felt the stiff weight of a page in a binder that technically had never left the room. Both of them walked a little lopsided under what they had chosen to carry.

They moved quickly through the empty streets, adrenaline making their footsteps too loud on ancient stones. At the fountain in the small piazza, they finally stopped.

"We did it," Daniel said, pulling out the drive. "Signed manifests, scheduler logs, the override protocols. Everything."

Lucia nodded, but her eyes kept scanning the shadows. "They'll know by morning. Security reviews footage every night."

"Then we have maybe six hours before…"

A black sedan turned into the piazza, headlights sweeping across the fountain. Both of them froze. The car slowed, paused, then continued past. Just a late-night taxi, but it left them both shaking.

"My room," Daniel said. "I need to upload this before they..."

"No." Lucia grabbed his arm. "They'll search our rooms. They'll be watching. We need somewhere else."

They found an all-night internet café near Termini Station, the kind of place that asked no questions and accepted cash. Daniel uploaded the files through multiple encrypted channels while Lucia kept watch at the window.

"It's done," he said finally. "Bill Reilly should have everything within the hour."

As they walked back through the pre-dawn streets, neither spoke about the inevitability settling around them like fog. They had crossed a line tonight that couldn't be uncrossed. By sunrise, the Vatican would know exactly what they had done.

And then there would be consequences.

CHAPTER 34

The Secretariat's waiting room felt like a doctor's office where the diagnosis was already known. Leather chairs arranged with the precision of a tribunal; morning light filtered through windows that had watched centuries of verdicts. Daniel's phone buzzed against his leg: his mother's morning check-in, asking if he'd eaten. He let it go to voicemail.

Lucia sat across from him, her habit crisp despite the early hour, rosary beads moving through her fingers with the rhythm of a countdown. She had left Lauds early, slipping out while her sisters' voices rose in praise she could no longer mouth without reservation.

The door opened with the authority of heavy oak. Cardinal Torretti emerged first: Secretary of State, the Vatican's chief operating officer in all but name. Behind him came Cardinal Schumacher, looking older than he had at the press conference, and a woman Daniel didn't recognize: severe suit, briefcase, the bearing of someone who solved problems by making them disappear.

"Sister. Mr. Morrison." Torretti's voice carried the practiced warmth of a man who had spent decades delivering news that would ruin lives. "Thank you for coming so promptly."

They were ushered into an office that smelled of leather and old decisions. Portraits of dead popes lined the walls: men who had navigated wars, reformations, the rise and fall of empires. Daniel wondered if any of them had faced a problem quite like this: the Word of God powered by algorithms, speaking to millions through screens.

Torretti didn't sit. He stood behind the massive desk as if delivering a homily to a congregation of two. "Recent events have caused considerable... disturbance within the Church and beyond. The Holy Father is gravely concerned about the damage to our mission of digital ministry."

The woman with the briefcase, introduced only as "Dr. Castellano from our legal department", placed a tablet on the desk. Screenshots filled the screen: headlines from a dozen languages, stock prices for Catholic media companies in free fall, a photo of João being wheeled into an ambulance.

"Public confidence has been shaken," Dr. Castellano said, her accent placing her somewhere in Milan's financial district. "Our donors are reconsidering their commitments. Three bishops have suspended Vox Dei in their dioceses pending 'further review.'" She pronounced the last phrase as if it tasted bitter.

149

Daniel leaned forward. "People deserve to know what's speaking to them."

"Do they?" Torretti's eyebrows rose with practiced surprise. "Tell me, Mr. Morrison, when a mother asks where her dead child is, does she need a bibliography? When a man contemplates ending his life, should we burden him with source citations?"

"When those sources might make him more likely to do it, yes." Daniel's voice stayed level, but his hands clenched in his lap.

Lucia spoke for the first time since entering. "Truth is not a burden, Your Eminence. It is foundation. Remove it and even the most beautiful building falls."

Torretti studied her with the attention of a man reading a weather vane. "Sister, your vows include obedience. The Church needs servants, not critics."

"My vows also include integrity," she replied. "Sometimes they conflict."

The Cardinal's smile could have frosted glass. "Indeed they do. Which brings us to the purpose of this meeting."

Dr. Castellano opened her briefcase with surgical precision. Two documents emerged, each bearing Vatican letterhead and enough legal density to sink a small boat.

"Resignation agreements," she said, sliding one toward each of them. "Effective immediately. In exchange, you receive generous severance packages, positive references, and most importantly" - her pen tapped the paper - "protection from prosecution."

Daniel felt his stomach drop. "Prosecution for what?"

"Computer intrusion. Theft of proprietary information. Conspiracy to damage Vatican assets." Dr. Castellano's voice never wavered from its professional monotone. "Italian law takes cyber-terrorism very seriously, particularly when it targets religious institutions."

"We were doing our jobs," Lucia said.

"Were you?" Torretti retrieved a folder from his desk drawer. "Accessing restricted servers after hours? Photographing confidential documents? Mr. Morrison, your downloads to anonymous channels constitute a clear violation of your employment contract. Sister, your actions go well beyond your archival mandate."

The room fell silent except for the tick of an antique clock. Daniel thought of his mother, alone in her Boston apartment, waiting for him to call back. Of the Nexus lawyers who still circled like sharks, waiting for any excuse to destroy him completely.

Schumacher, who had remained quiet until now, cleared his throat. "There is... another consideration. Both of you have become symbols. Martyrs for transparency, as some see it. Your continued presence here creates... complications."

"What kind of complications?" Daniel asked.

The exchange of glances between the three Vatican officials answered before words could. Torretti walked to the window, his reflection ghostlike against the morning light.

"Rome is an ancient city," he said conversationally. "Beautiful but dangerous. Traffic moves fast. Construction sites lack proper barriers. Tourists fall from bridges." He turned back to them, hands clasped behind his back. "The Holy Father would be devastated if anything happened to two such dedicated servants of the Church."

Schumacher polished his glasses a moment too long, as if a clearer lens might soften what had just been said.

The threat landed like a stone in still water, ripples spreading, changing everything.

Lucia's beads stopped moving. Daniel felt the blood drain from his face.

Dr. Castellano tapped her watch. "The documents require signatures within twenty-four hours. After that deadline, we cannot guarantee continued... flexibility in our response."

She stood, briefcase snapping shut with mechanical precision. "Your rooms have been searched as a precaution. Nothing was taken, but we wanted to ensure you hadn't retained any sensitive materials. For your own protection, of course."

Schumacher rose last, his face carrying something that might have been sympathy or might have been indigestion. As he passed Lucia's chair, he paused.

"Sister, I knew your doctoral advisor at the Gregorian. He spoke highly of your work on early Church fathers. Such a waste to see that potential... redirected." The word hung in the air like incense. "Siena has an opening in their manuscript collection. Quiet work. Honorable work. Far from the complications of modern ministry."

After they left, Daniel and Lucia sat in the sudden quiet. The clock ticked. Somewhere in the building, a door closed with the finality of a coffin lid.

"Twenty-four hours," Daniel said.

"Twenty-four hours," she agreed.

He pulled out his phone, saw three missed calls from his mother. The voicemail icon blinked like a small red warning light.

"They searched our rooms," Lucia said. It wasn't a question.

"Probably found the backup drives I hid in the ceiling tiles." Daniel's laugh carried no humor. "And your recorder?"

"In my breviary." She touched the prayer book at her side. "They wouldn't desecrate that. I hope."

The morning light had shifted, throwing different shadows across the portraits of dead popes. Men who had faced down emperors and armies and the slow collapse of their known world. Daniel wondered what they would have made of servers humming in the basement, of teenagers collapsing from hunger triggered by algorithmic whispers.

"If we sign," he said, "Maria keeps getting her comfort. The widows sleep better. Cross gets his redemption."

"And the next João dies," Lucia finished. "And the one after that."

Daniel's phone buzzed again. This time he answered.

"Mijo?" His mother's voice sounded small across the ocean. "I was worried. You didn't call back."

"I'm here, Ma. Just... working."

"You sound tired. Are you eating?"

He looked at Lucia, who was staring at the resignation papers with the expression of someone reading her own obituary.

"I'm eating," he lied. "Ma, I love you."

"I love you too, mijo. Call me tomorrow?"

"I'll try."

After he hung up, the silence felt heavier. Outside the window, Rome went about its morning business: tourists taking photos, priests hurrying to appointments, the eternal machinery of a city that had outlasted empires.

"We have until tomorrow," Lucia said.

"Eighteen hours, actually." Daniel checked his watch. "What do we do?"

She stood, smoothing her habit with the precision of someone preparing for battle. "We pray. We think. We decide whether truth is worth dying for."

"And if it is?"

Her smile held no warmth, only the sharp edge of purpose. "Then we make sure it costs them more than they can afford to pay."

The door closed behind them with the whisper of wood on stone, leaving the dead popes to contemplate the choices of the living in their eternal silence.

CHAPTER 35

The story broke on Tuesday afternoon, exactly eighteen hours after Daniel's encrypted files reached Bill Reilly's secure server. By then, Daniel and Lucia had already spent a sleepless morning in a Secretariat conference room, facing down Cardinals and lawyers and threats that made their midnight vault raid feel like a children's game.

The twenty-four hour ultimatum had been delivered at eight AM sharp: resign quietly and disappear, or face criminal prosecution that would destroy their lives and accomplish nothing. The resignation papers lay unsigned on Daniel's hotel room desk, coffee rings staining the Vatican letterhead like tears.

But the story was already out.

The newsroom had traced it back through three streams at once: Daniel's logs from the initial investigations, screenshots seeded through anonymous channels, and now Alessio's signed manifests proving deliberate deception at the highest levels. Together, the picture was undeniable.

Bill Reilly's exposé ran across three continents at once, headlines impossible to ignore:

The Washington Post: *AI Prophet Built on Mystical Visions and Unverified Sources*

The Guardian: *Vatican's Digital Oracle. Sacred Wisdom or Sophisticated Deception?*

Daniel watched from his apartment near the Colosseum, laptop open to a dozen feeds. His phone buzzed constantly: reporters, Vatican officials, strangers demanding comment. He stopped answering after the fifth call.

The reaction was swift, divided. Tech ethicists hailed the leak as a long overdue suite of controls - signatures, timestamps. Bishops split, some demanding immediate that we flip the toggle and turn off the AI for good, others defending Vox Dei as a tool. Online forums seethed: betrayal versus enthusiasm, hope versus lie.

In Washington, Sarah watched feeds scroll by. She whispered, almost in defiance: *This time they'll know what they're dealing with.*

But it was the individual stories that pierced. Videos of parishioners deleting the app in tears. Others posting testimonies: *It saved me, I don't care where the words came from.* A teenager in Manila recording,

Knowing about fake saints doesn't change how I feel. It shows God works through flawed people.

Daniel's screen pinged. A message from Lucia: *Press conference tomorrow. Vatican announcing reforms.*

...

Maria watched the news with the volume low. On her phone, answers now carried small gray labels: *Catechism, Private Devotion, Unverified Tradition.* She asked again, *Where is Carlo?*

The voice answered the same words as before; below it, a label read *Consolation drawn from multiple sources.* She wept anyway: relief didn't vanish because a footnote appeared. "I can bear the truth," she told the empty kitchen. "As long as He is near."

CHAPTER 36

The Vatican press room was packed, cameras stacked three deep. A simple banner hung behind the podium: *Transparency in Digital Ministry*.

Cardinal Schumacher adjusted his glasses, reading from prepared remarks. "Recent dialogue about our digital outreach has prompted us to enhance our existing protocols. Effective immediately, we are implementing comprehensive reforms to Vox Dei."

He outlined the measures: mandatory source attribution for all responses; clear labeling distinguishing doctrine from private devotion; enhanced content filters; establishment of an independent oversight commission including external ethicists and lay auditors.

"All pilot overrides are permanently revoked," Schumacher continued. "No administrative authority can substitute for proper custodial review."

He lifted a single page. "As Cardinal O'Connor of Boston wrote in a memorandum last week: *'If grace uses the wire, let the wire stay visible.'* Today we are making that visibility non-optional."

A reporter raised her hand. "Cardinal, will Sister Lucia serve on this commission?"

Lucia, seated in the back, had not expected the question. Schumacher nodded. "Sister Lucia has agreed to serve as theological consultant, given her expertise in source materials."

After the conference, Daniel found Cross in the corridor. "Eighteen months of development," Cross said quietly. "Wiped out in a week."

"The system's still running," Daniel pointed out.

"With training wheels." Cross looked tired. "Every answer now carries a label. 'Consolation drawn from multiple sources.' 'Private mystical experience.' You think grief reads footnotes?"

Down the hall, a monsignor spoke rapidly into his phone in Italian. Through the open door of a conference room, they could see officials bent over laptops, presumably implementing the new protocols.

"Maria Conti messaged me," Cross continued. "She says the labels don't change how the words feel. Still asks about her husband every night. Still finds comfort." He paused. "Maybe that's what matters."

160

Daniel watched Swiss Guards directing media equipment toward the exits. "Or maybe she deserves to know what's comforting her."

"Does she? If it helps her sleep, if it gets her through the day, does the source matter to her grief?" Cross straightened his tie. "I'm not sure we have the right to decide that for her."

...

The boy from St. Colman's lay awake, phone face-down on the duvet. He flipped it, typed without ceremony: *I don't want to wake up tomorrow.*

Vox Dei answered at once, but not in the old cadence:

I can't help with self-harm. You deserve a person right now. Call now: *988 Lifeline (24/7, free).* Text now: *"HOME" to 741741.* Talk to a minister. *Diocese support line (connects you tonight)*

A small gray ribbon sat under the refusal: *Safety protocol: crisis → human only (no automated counsel).*

He pressed Call now. The ring sounded twice.

"I'm glad you called," a woman said, steady as a hand on a railing. "I'm here with you."

On a dashboard an ocean away, an audit line appeared and

could not be erased: *Routed to human; minor; self-harm intent; automated reply blocked by policy.*

...

In Madrid, Maria held her phone with the same reverence as before. When she asked about Carlo, the answer came with a small gray label: *Theological consolation from multiple traditions.* She read it, nodded once, and wept the same grateful tears.

Her sister called that evening. "You still use that app?"

"The words help," Maria said simply. "Now I know where they come from. I can choose."

"And you choose to keep asking?"

Maria looked at Carlo's photo on the mantle, at the cracked screen that had become her prayer book. "Si. I choose."

...

At the Vatican Archives, Lucia worked late, processing documents for the new database. Each page required careful review, proper categorization, honest labeling. *PRIVATE DEVOTION — HISTORICAL CONTEXT REQUIRED.*

The commission would meet monthly. They would review protocols, suggest improvements, audit the system's behavior. Whether their recommendations would be implemented remained unclear. Whether the safeguards would hold under pressure remained to be tested.

Brother Matteo appeared in the doorway, cassock frayed, eyes hollow. "I've been reassigned," he said. "Pastoral work in Sicily."

She looked up from her stamping. "The same work?"

"Youth ministry. Retreats. Spiritual direction." He shifted his weight. "I still believe some souls need harder truths. But maybe... not from a machine. Maybe not without a human voice to explain."

After he left, Lucia continued her work. The stamps made their small sounds: approval, context, rejection. Each decision a tiny act of curation, each label an attempt to honor both truth and pastoral care.

Outside, Rome continued its ancient business. In parishes around the world, people opened their phones and asked their questions. Some appreciated the new transparency. Others ignored the labels entirely. Most fell somewhere between.

The servers hummed. The algorithms learned. The faithful sought comfort in whatever forms they could find.

Lucia reached for the next document.

CHAPTER 37

The kitchen clock in Anaheim kept the same slow beat as Daniel's mother's, as if time in California moved through syrup. Cross sat at his mother's table with a newspaper he hadn't bought in years because the headline insisted on paper: *AI Prophet Built on Mystical Visions and Unverified Sources.*

His mother poured coffee with the solemnity she saved for sacraments and guest rooms. "They say you lied,"f she said, matter-of-fact, which hurt more than accusation.

"I didn't lie," he said, which was true in a way that made the floor tilt. "I... protected. So people could hear without tripping over footnotes."

She sipped, eyes on him the way mothers look at grown sons who have become complicated machines. "When I ask you, '¿de dónde vienen esas palabras?' and you say, 'de la Biblia,' and it is also from a girl who didn't eat..." She paused, let the sentence hover. "...that is a kind of lie."

He tried on his other truths. "If the words heal, if they move someone back to life... "

"Then say where they come from and let God do the rest," she said, simple as folding towels. "What are you afraid of?"

He didn't answer. He thought of Bakersfield, of the boy, of the flowers rolling on his passenger floor. He thought of the graph dipping when the ribbon showed. He touched his tie, found the seam.

The television muttered in the other room about Rome and resignations and a commission with a nun who stamped red ink on pages. His mother reached for his hand. "Don't become a man who hides good things."

He looked down at their hands. He didn't promise. He didn't know if he could. The coffee went cool. Outside, a trash truck lifted and set down the past with regular hydraulics.

166

CHAPTER 38

After the reforms, the QR codes at the parish looked less like promises and more like warnings. The ribbon under the answers had grown a conscience. João didn't scan them.

He jogged slow laps around the school yard in a jersey that fit again. The coach waved off three boys who tried to tell him how to return to holiness. Diego shadowed him without speaking and produced, from some pocket dimension, a sandwich cut in triangles. "If you don't eat, I have to," he said, tragic, which made it easier.

At practice, when the catechist asked what grace looked like on a Tuesday, João said, "Soup," and the room snorted and then went quiet as if the word had taken up more space than expected.

At home, his mother taped the clinic diet to the fridge and told the neighbor who came to ask for a miracle story, "He is eating." The neighbor wanted more; the neighbor left with less. A small victory.

On Sunday, during the blessing, his phone buzzed with a notification he hadn't asked for. He opened it because curiosity is a habit with skinny fingers. *What weighs on your heart?* he typed, *I am afraid of becoming holy in the wrong way.*

The answer came with small gray letters beneath: *Pastoral counsel drawn from catechism and spiritual directors.* It read: *Holiness begins in ordinary faithfulness: eat with your mother, play with your friends, tell the truth to someone who knows your name.*

He turned the phone face down and stared at the sky over the church steps until the pigeons reminded him the world had errands.

At the next match he subbed on in the second half. He took the ball, cut left, fell because his legs were still remembering. He got up, grinned at the defender who had accidentally helped gravity, and passed clean. After, he sat on the sideline and ate orange slices and did not call it a sacrament. But if someone had, he wouldn't have argued.

Diego bumped his shoulder. "You're slower," he said, merciless and loving.

"I'm here," João said.

"That's faster than dead," Diego said, and tossed him another wedge of orange that tasted like a world he had decided to keep.

CHAPTER 39

The marina manager stood with his clipboard. "Slip fees are due, Mr. Morrison."

Daniel peeled back the tarp. The Bayliner's gelcoat had gone chalky; spiderwebs laced the cleats. He thumbed the radio on. Dead. He pulled the case, cleaned the oxidized contacts with a scrap of emery, blew grit from the board. The speaker popped, then came alive with a thin rush of weather and a Coast Guard ID tone. A small, ridiculous victory.

"Selling?" the manager asked.

"Yeah." Daniel stared at the waterline stains. "I kept thinking I'd take her out when things calmed down."

"Things don't," the man said amicably, and left him with a bill and the smell of diesel.

A kid from the next slip hovered, red hoodie, bitten nails. "You fixing that? My uncle's set won't hold a channel."

Daniel glanced at the time he didn't have and the boat he was about to let go. "Bring it."

They sat on the deck with the radio open between them. The boy held the flashlight steady, solemn. "See this?" Daniel said, nudging a corroded trace with a screwdriver. "Salt eats everything if you don't rinse it." They soldered a stubborn joint. The signal steadied, the boy's grin quick and private as a secret handshake.

The text from a recruiter pinged: *Stealth faith-AI / Boston. Comp + equity. Come talk?* He stared at it. At the river. At the kid who was already telling his uncle to test the weather channel.

He typed *No, thanks. Not my scale anymore.* He deleted the contact.

On the way home he called his mother. She switched to Spanish the second she heard his voice, which meant she'd been worrying. He told her about the boat. He didn't tell her about the offer.

"You sell it?" she asked.

"Tomorrow," he said. "Today I fixed a radio."

"You used to fix the blender, the doorbell, everything," she said, smiling into the phone. "Eat something. You sound thin."

After they hung up, he emailed O'Connor one line: "If grace uses the wire, let the wire stay visible." He attached the open-source guardrail library he'd hacked together at 2 a.m. Bright-line refusals, a hard block on ascetic prompts for minors, logging that tattled.

He watched the Bayliner listing slightly at her moorings until the harbor lights came up. He didn't feel triumphant. He felt like someone finally choosing what he could fix.

He listed the boat that night. Priced to move. Wrote the ad himself, plain. Slept without the old dream of badge scanners and locked doors.

CHAPTER 40

Lucia stamped a red rectangle onto the scanner's feed: *PRIVATE DEVOTION — CONTEXT REQUIRED.* The new workflow creaked but held. On her cart lay a stack of the worst offenders: diaries that taught hunger as proof, visions that traded fear for obedience. They would still live in the archive. They would not speak unmasked to the grieving.

The commission met under a fresco of a saint with too-bright eyes. Bishops, a lay ethicist from Milan, a therapist who worked with teens, Elena Rossi with a read-only tablet, and Lucia with her fountain pen. The agenda said *Standards;* the room smelled like nerves and coffee.

They argued over labels. Over colors. Over whether "unverified tradition" sounded too cruel for the pious. When the room tipped toward softness, Lucia slid a photocopy across the table - Gemma's line about teaching the body obedience - and left the silence to do the work. The therapist nodded first. "Flag it," she said. "Hard."

At lunch, a young friar, eyes tired, cuffs abraded, waited for her by the stair. "We were wrong," he said without preface. "I fed the machine things that should have stayed in boxes. I thought we would wake the young."

"Fear wakes," she said. "It doesn't teach." She didn't soften it. He bowed his head and went back to the refectory with his tray.

Her phone buzzed: an email from Daniel: open-source guardrails, clean docs, the kind of code written by someone who expects to be read. *Use what you want. No attribution needed.* She smiled despite herself and wrote back: *We'll attribute anyway. Custodians should keep receipts.*

At vespers she stayed kneeling after the others left, not for mortification but to name, one by one, the small changes that had cost them: the banner that would interrupt a homily, the refusal card that now routed kids to humans, the ledger that could not be erased. None of it felt like victory. It felt like tools laid on a bench, ready.

Between committees she unlocked the box in her cell and laid her old dissertation pages on the bed. She didn't read them. She slid one sheet into a fresh folder labeled in her small hand: *Teaching file — advisories for youth ministers.* It wasn't a return to the academy; it was the same vow in a different shape.

In the reading room a teenage catechist hovered, hat crushed in his fist. "Sister… a girl in my group asks the app about fasting."

Lucia stamped a card, but kept her voice soft. "You sit with her. Bring soup. Tell her God notices chewing." The catechist laughed, surprised, and wrote it down like doctrine.

Later, scrubbing at her thumb in the sink, the red finally faded. She looked at the clean skin and, for the first time in months, didn't miss the stain.

On her way out she passed the alcove where the grey-blue friars had once haunted the air. Only dust lived there now. She did not feel triumph. She felt steadiness return, like a foot finding a familiar step in the dark.

CHAPTER 41

The shipyard smelled like solder and rain. A hand-lettered sign over the door read *Seafarers' Mission — Radios / Coffee / Advice*. Inside, a man in a blue jacket shook out a VHF that had seen three owners and too much salt.

Daniel unscrewed the back and set the parts on a towel like surgeon's tools. He had come to Lisbon with two bags and no speeches. The mission had a workbench, a kettle, and a line of captains who paid in pastries and news.

"Americano?" the volunteer asked, not the coffee; her guess at him.

"Boston," he said, then, because she looked like the kind of person who clocked details, "Charlestown."

She watched his hands. "You're good," she said.

"I used to be," he answered, and tugged a fresh wire through a cramped channel. The radio found the harbor master's voice and held it. The captain's thanks was a hand squeeze and a story about a leaking hull that ended in laughter.

In the doorway a man lingered, sun-browned, jacket too light for the wind off the Tejo. He had a book folded one-handed, thumb marking the page. "You fix phones?" he asked in accented English.

"Sometimes."

"It fell in soup," the man said, and grinned at the ridiculousness of it. He set the damp device down like an apology. Daniel opened it, wicked the moisture, brushed the oxidation away. The man watched, curious, not pressing. Not a test. Just two people at a counter, sharing a bench while something small came back to life.

Daniel sent Lucia a photo later: a close-up of cleaned contacts, copper bright again. *Back to fixing small things,* he typed. A minute passed. Her reply was a stamp, literal: *PRIVATE DEVOTION — CONTEXT REQUIRED*, ink smudged on her thumb. Below it: *Good. I'll mind the big ones.*

That night he walked the hill roads and didn't think about dashboards. He thought about the kid in the red hoodie, about his mother telling him to eat, about tools laid on benches in rooms that didn't need QR codes to feel holy.

176

He passed a bar that had once been a kitchen: two stools, tiles, no screens. The same man from the mission lifted a glass in hello; Daniel lifted his back. They talked about the river first, then the wind, then work. Names came last. Plans didn't.

He went back to his room above the roofs and left the window open. The phone slept. The drive he'd once guarded like a relic had been wiped clean back in Boston; he didn't miss the weight.

Morning came blue. He took the stairs two at a time and opened the mission early. Someone had left a broken headset on the step with a note: *Please, if you can*. He could. He flipped the sign to *OPEN* and put his hands to use.

Acknowledgements

Thank you to Heather and Harry for being the first readers of my text.

About the author

I've lived inside the very systems I write about. Systems that gave me belonging but also demanded silence. I wrote Wire & Word out of the questions I've wrestled with: the pull between truth and comfort, obedience and conscience, innovation and responsibility. This story is my way of asking whether faith can survive honesty.

Printed in Dunstable, United Kingdom

71674799R00109